I0648490

Alexander McLean

Tribute to the memory of John B. Skinner

Alexander McLean

Tribute to the memory of John B. Skinner

ISBN/EAN: 9783743376144

Manufactured in Europe, USA, Canada, Australia, Japa

Cover: Foto ©Andreas Hilbeck / pixelio.de

Manufactured and distributed by brebook publishing software
(www.brebook.com)

Alexander McLean

Tribute to the memory of John B. Skinner

TRIBUTE

TO

The Memory

OF

JOHN B. SKINNER

CONTAINING A

BRIEF ACCOUNT OF HIS LAST ILLNESS, DEATH, AND FUNERAL OBSEQUIES,

WITH

A SERMON BY REV. ALEX. McLEAN.

ALSO :

ACTION OF THE SESSION OF CALVARY CHURCH, MEETING
OF THE BAR OF ERIE COUNTY, RESOLUTIONS AND
MEMORIALS, OBITUARY NOTICES OF
THE PRESS, ETC. ;

AND

A MEMORIAL PAPER PREPARED FOR THE HISTORICAL SOCIETY,
BY THE HON. JAMES O. PUTNAM.

BUFFALO, N. Y.

PRINTING HOUSE OF MATTHEWS & WARREN,
Office of the "Buffalo Commercial Advertiser,"

1874.

Father, I will that they also, whom thou hast given me, be with me where I am: that they may behold my glory, which thou hast given me.—St. JOHN xvii. 24.

If we believe that Jesus died and rose again, even so them also which sleep in Jesus will God bring with him.— 1 THESS. iv. 14.

It shall come to pass, that at evening time it shall be light.—ZECH. xiv. 7.

OBITUARY.

·

JOHN B. SKINNER was born at Williamstown, Mass., July 23, 1799, and died at his residence in Buffalo, June 6, 1871.

Although he had lived more than three-score and ten years, he felt none of the infirmities of age until within a few months of his last illness.

Early in the Spring of 1871 he seemed conscious of increasing debility. His step was less quick and elastic, and the long walks to which he had ever been accustomed were gradually shortened.

The last Sabbath in April he attended church as usual, and on Wednesday dined with his family, at the house of his brother-in-law; but the next morning was unable to rise. Drs. Rochester and White were called at once to his bedside, but found symptoms of prostration so alarming that they entertained little hope of his recovery. At times he seemed better, and during the latter part of May was able to drive out nearly every day for a week.

On Friday, June 2, he was much worse, and from that time declined rapidly. Monday night his sleep was quiet and restful, and so continued the following day until evening, when he gently breathed his life away.

On Friday following, at 3 P. M., appropriate funeral services were held at his late residence, and largely attended, many of his old friends, members of the Bar and others, from adjoining counties, being present. The Rev. Alex. McLean, his pastor, conducted the services, assisted by Rev. A. T. Chester, D. D., Rev. Grosvenor W. Heacock, D. D., and Rev. Erskine N. White.

The following gentlemen were in attendance as pall-bearers:

Hon. Millard Fillmore,	Hon. N. K. Hall,
" Geo. W. Clinton,	" I. A. Verplanck,
" R. P. Marvin,	" J. S. Ganson,
" W. H. Greene,	" S. S. Rogers.

The remains were placed temporarily in the crypt of St. Paul's Cathedral, and subsequently removed to the family Mausoleum, at Forest Lawn.

"FATHER."

AT "FOREST LAWN."

Let sculptured wreath of laurel twine the name
We hold more precious as the years go by:
This much we give the world, his meed of fame,
Whose royal nature trembled at a sigh;
Tender, compassionate, just, wise and good,
He filled the measure of his earthly days:
Heroic in his purpose, firm he stood,
And State and Church unite to speak his praise.
Yet dearer far to us the cherished name
Which made the Home the centre of our bliss,
How fondly spoken as we bent to claim
The morning welcome and the evening kiss.
We know not what new name to him is given,
But "Father" we would call our loved in Heaven.

E. M. OLMSTED.

LE ROY, Nov. 10, 1873.

SERMON.

PROFESSIONAL SUCCESS NOT INCOMPATIBLE WITH WHOLE-HEARTED DEVOTION TO THE SERVICE OF CHRIST.

NOT SLOTHFUL IN BUSINESS; FERVENT IN SPIRIT; SERVING THE LORD.
—*Romans* xii. 11.

Life is a problem, its true solution an absolute impossibility only as we are assisted by the teachings of Revelation. We have manifestly interests of an earthly character which cannot be disregarded, and just as manifestly other interests which are spiritual and eternal; to neglect which must be in the highest degree culpable. To live in this world at all, we must of necessity devote much of our time to its pursuits. This, indeed, is one of the conditions of the present, from which there is no escape. The law of labor is imperative. The body has its wants which cannot be disregarded, and the provision for these wants is the reward of indefatigable labor. Business therefore becomes a necessity. But since we are also immortal beings, endowed with a spiritual nature, man cannot live by bread alone, no more than he can live without bread. We cannot, therefore, devote ourselves exclusively to either the one part of our complex nature or the other, and either be happy or fulfil life's great end.

He is a fool,—and is so characterized by the Great Teacher Himself,—who, devoting all his time and efforts merely to the body, and having at last gained the wherewithal to satisfy its wants, says, "Soul, thou hast much goods laid up for many years; take thine ease; eat, drink and be merry:" as if, by any possibility, the soul could be satisfied with these things. He is a coward who, in view of the strong temptation to neglect the soul's interests for those of the body, cuts himself loose from society, ignoring all its claims and responsibilities, and fleeing into solitude, devotes himself exclusively to his eternal interests.

The very sublimity of the present life consists in its complex relations, and in so keeping the mastery over them that apparently conflicting interests are harmonized and each kept in its own place; the work allotted to us here prosecuted with becoming diligence, while the soul is kept as a sacred altar upon which the fire of fervent devotion is ever burning.

We know of no other order of intelligences, circumstanced as we are, who have to hold the balance of temporal and eternal interests with an even hand, and carry the clue of rectitude through all the labyrinth of conflicting interests. The nice adjustment of these interests has been made a subject of special revelation. Our earthly duties are unfolded, our eternal relations disclosed, and the important issues which depend upon the manner in which we discharge the trust committed to us, are clearly set forth. Our text is a complete summary of the duties required of us : "Not slothful in business; fervent in spirit; serving the Lord." The first clause, "Not slothful in business," is very comprehensive, including not merely what we designate by the word business, but every duty which presents itself. It is the exhortation of the wise man condensed into a single expression,—"Whatsoever thy hands find to do, do it with thy might." The second clause of our text sets forth the spirit which is to animate this activity—whole-hearted devotion to the work committed to us; while the last clause reveals the true inspiration to such a life—"Serve the Lord." The active labor, of whatever kind it may be, the toil of our hands or the labor of our minds, is to be service rendered to the Lord; while the fervent spirit of devotion is to be continually ascending like sweet smelling incense to His throne. The whole life is thus to be made a sacrifice and a service, "holy and acceptable to God."

We all admit that this is a very difficult requirement. It is the ideal of a perfect life. In Christ alone have we its perfect realization. Those who approximate nearest to it are most like Him. To copy His example perfectly would be to obey perfectly the exhortation of the text. He neglected no duty for the sake of devoting Himself more exclusively to other, and what might have been regarded as higher, duties. It mattered not whether He was occupied in the carpenter's shop at Nazareth, or was preaching upon the mountain's side to a great multitude. In the one place as well as in the other He was "about His Father's business."

It is no uncommon thing to see the first part of this injunction carried out to the very letter; especially in the restricted sense in which it is commonly regarded, as referring exclusively to earthly pursuits. There is but little need in this day to give from the pulpit any exhortations to incite to diligence in business. The pressure is all in this direction. Yea, so great has this become, that every year many give way under the mighty strain to which their powers are subjected, and fall as victims to undue devotion to business. They even make this an excuse for neglecting higher interests. They say, "Let us attend to one thing at a time. We will be diligent in business till we have secured a fortune; after that we will be fervent in spirit, devoting the remainder of our lives to the service of the Lord." You know how worthless all such promises are, how delusive are such hopes. The man who devotes the best years of his life to purely business pursuits, dwarfs his whole nature and unfits himself for higher walks of usefulness.

It is very rarely, indeed, that we can point to any man as an example of a higher and nobler life, and by his marked success, even in a worldly point of view, show that the service of God is not incompatible with at least a satisfactory degree of temporal prosperity. In some cases the Christian character is not so decided as to leave no room for doubt, while in others the measure of success attained is so meagre as to furnish no very strong incentive to induce others to copy the example. So that we have mainly to rely upon the abstract truth when we would show that it is possible to be "not slothful in business," and yet "fervent in spirit; serving the Lord."

But to-day I can present the truth, not merely by precept but also by example. A life has just closed, so far as respects this world, which is well calculated to teach us that success in a laborious, fascinating and absorbing profession is not incompatible with whole-hearted devotion to the service of Christ. Before its lustre fades away, I would impress its lessons, and, if possible, induce some of you to copy this example.

This sacred hour should not be spent in empty eulogy upon a fallible mortal like ourselves. The Holy Spirit in the inspired word teaches us by example. Yet carefully refraining from everything like this, I would magnify not the man but the grace of God which made him what he was. None was more conscious than our departed friend whose loss we mourn, that he was a debtor to Divine grace for all that he was and for all that he accomplished during a life which just passed beyond the common limit of three-score years and ten. He arrogated nothing to himself. He was like a child in his unassuming modesty, and like a child in his tenderly sympathetic nature. A more sensitive and loving heart I never knew.

This was a natural gift, inherited no doubt from his ancestors. His emotional nature was just the counterpart of his delicate and highly organized physical constitution.

With the same tenderness as if he were present, would I speak of him to-day, and therefore my endeavor will be not to say a single word that would have wounded his modesty. Yea, may he not be here with his sainted daughter and others who have gone from this communion to the higher fellowship of the glorified, although we shall see their faces no more. I feel as if even now he were looking upon me from his accustomed place, with those eyes which were always dimmed with tears whenever a Saviour's love was presented, and by his earnest looks was saying, " Not *me*, but *Christ.*"

Not thee, but Christ, my brother, shall be the subject of this discourse. But surely, since now thou art *with Christ*, we who are still left may show what Christ did *for* thee and *by* thee. No wreath would we entwine for thy brow, since already thy Master has placed there the "crown of life." But we would show how He made thee a jewel fit for His own glorious crown. We would speak of thee only as the Holy Spirit has spoken of those who "through faith and patience inherited the promises;" to show that the same grace has still the same power over those who yield themselves to its influence. It was this which enabled thee to approximate so nearly to the ideal of a perfect life as described in our text, "Not slothful in business; fervent in spirit; serving the Lord."

Let us, brethren and friends, glance at his life, that we may learn what appears to me to be its chief lesson, viz: that it is possible to be diligent and successful in a professional career, and yet "fervent in spirit; serving the Lord."

The Hon. John B. Skinner was a grandson of the Rev. Thomas Skinner, a graduate of Harvard College, whose whole ministerial life was spent in Westchester, Conn., as pastor of the Congregational church in that place. His father,

Benj. Skinner, removed to Williamstown, Mass., and took a very active part in the organization and building of Williams College, which has for years occupied such a commanding position among our New England literary institutions. It was in this place that the subject of this sketch was born. He enjoyed the highest literary advantages this country then afforded, and so diligently improved them that he was admitted to college when only fifteen years of age, graduating with honor and high promise of future usefulness when a mere youth of nineteen. The following three years were devoted by him to the study of his chosen profession. With such zeal did he apply himself, aided by the most famous instructors, both public and private, that at the age of twenty-two he was admitted to the Supreme Court of the State of New York.

Frequently have I heard him speak of the thorough preparation required in those days, in comparison with the meagre attainments which are sometimes regarded as sufficient now, for admission into this honorable and important profession. His whole future success, with his accustomed modesty, he attributed to his thorough preparation and not to his own native abilities.

There was a sad scene through which he passed about this time, which made a deep and permanent impression upon his young mind. His father, feeling that death was at hand, like good old Jacob, called his sons around his dying bed and prayed for them, one after another, by name, earnestly pleading for those who had not yet given evidence that they were truly converted, that they might be included in the covenant of grace. But when he came to John, he prayed for him as if he were already a child of God. The godly father doubtless detected in his blameless life and tender regard for sacred things, the commencement of that work of grace which was to become deeper and deeper, till it resulted in that high Christian character with which we are familiar.

Soon after his admission to the bar, he sought a field of labor in what was then the far West, and settled in an adjoining county. Although only a boy, he was at once engaged in some of the most important cases then before the courts. Responsibility was forced upon him rather than courted. I remember well how graphically he described his feelings when called upon, I think by the appointment of the Court, to defend a man who was upon trial for his life. Never did a young physician, in treating a critical case, have greater anxiety for the life of his patient than this young barrister had for the life of his client. He felt that he held the poor man's destiny in his hand, and was almost overwhelmed with the responsibility. His pathetic eloquence prevailed, and his client was acquitted. This at once established his reputation. Business rolled in upon him, till in a few years, if a dispute arose among neighbors in any of the counties in which he practiced, the effort was who should first reach Squire Skinner's office and secure his services. The one who was successful in this felt that his case was already won.

The labor which he performed during the first ten or fifteen years of his professional career was truly astounding. At the present rates for legal services, his income would have been at least a competence, if not a modest fortune.

But his efforts were not confined to the mere routine of professional duties. He took a deep interest in the political issues of the day, and had he been ambitious for political distinction, he might have aspired successfully to far higher offices than any which he filled with such honor and distinction ; for he honored the position, rather than deriving honor from the position. His effort was rather to keep out of office than to secure it. This feature of his public life inspired the confidence which he enjoyed, not merely among his political friends, but also opponents. Although devotedly attached to the political party which he espoused at the very beginning of his public life, and whose ranks he never deserted, yet he was not a party man for the emoluments of office, but from the honest conviction that its principles, if carried out, would secure the highest good for the whole country.

I never heard of but one charge brought against him, when a candidate for office, by the opposing party, and that he related to me himself. He was charged with having purchased a mortgage against a poor widow, turning her out of house and home. It was either the wilful or ignorant misrepresentation of an act of charity on his part. The widow consulted with him, and as the only way of securing her little property free from encumbrance, he had the mortgage foreclosed, that the property might be bought in for the widow herself, although I believe he was ostensibly the purchaser. This he related merely as an illustration of the misrepresentation to which the character of public men is exposed, in the excitement of a political campaign.

The habits of industry which he acquired continued through his whole life. While a member of Assembly for three successive terms, the last two being elected by both parties, his time was fully occupied. Being so universally known in this part of the State, if any important bill relative to local interests was to be presented, the labor of drafting it was always committed to him. And yet he found time to attend to other and higher interests for the good of the people. Intemperance then, as now, was the curse of the country; but the habit of moderate drink was then so general that few could be found to raise their voice against the consequent evil. While attending the Assembly, at Albany, with Chancellor Walworth he originated the first temperance meeting held in this State, and had the honor of being its presiding officer. I think that meeting was addressed by Rev. Dr. Hewit, the American apostle of temperance. Shortly after returning to his home, he visited every town in his own county, advocating this then unpopular cause, with so much success that an almost complete reformation was effected, the blessed fruits of which the County of Wyoming still enjoys.

When called to the bench as Judge, he was strict and impartial in his decisions, yet allowing the counsel who appeared before him great latitude in the management of their cases. This resulted from the discomfiture of a Judge of his acquaintance, who adopted just the opposite extreme. He had interrupted an advocate in his examination of a witness repeatedly, and at last, when the question was asked, "Was it moonlight the night when this event occurred?" the Judge wholly lost his patience, and said, "The time of the Court cannot be wasted by such irrelevant questions. What difference can it make in this case whether it was moonlight or not?" Soon the counsel showed that the whole case turned upon that very point. "This," said our friend, "I always remembered whenever inclined to lose my patience upon the bench, presuming that the counsel who had investigated the whole case knew better than I did the bearing of their questions."

I need not speak of the honor and distinction which he gained in his profession. His name is a household word in the county where his active professional life was passed. No man will be missed more, and no man mourned with greater sincerity. Few have had a more successful career. Had he coveted higher honors, they were easily within his reach. But instead of this he retired from active business when his powers were in full vigor; not, however, merely to enjoy the elegant leisure which he had earned by years of unremitting industry. His usefulness continued to the close of his life. Every important public charity in this and adjoining counties coveted his services. Nor did he accept these appointments as merely honorary. With as much fidelity as if they were his own personal interests did he serve these institutions.

It is only a very few months ago that he was sent for to Warsaw, to advocate the claims of a Reformatory upon a new plan, for those who had just entered upon a career of crime. His health was even then giving way. Those who heard him upon that occasion, and who had listened to his eloquence in times past, acknowledged that he surpassed his own happiest efforts. He related his experience as a lawyer, and said, "I throw my forty years of experience in the Courts of this State in favor of this movement. I know the corrupting influence of association with hardened criminals, upon those who have only taken the first steps in wrong doing. Provide for them such an asylum as this, and they may yet retrieve their characters and become useful members of society. Send them to our State prisons, and most of them are ruined forever. 'Evil communications corrupt good manners.' "

Truly he was "not slothful in business." "Whatsoever his hands found to do, he did it with all his might."

But were this all that could be said of him, although his was a successful life, according to a worldly standard, for he secured both fame and fortune, and yet maintained his character without a blot, so that a distinguished Judge of our own city in a single sentence pronounced the highest possible eulogy upon him, while we were together in the house of mourning, in these words: "He lies there just as pure as he was in his cradle;" yet, according to a higher standard, his life would have been divested of its chief glory; for all these things he might have done for profit or renown, merely for that honor which cometh from men. But he had higher views of life. His devotion to his profession and to public interests did not prevent him from devoting himself to the service of Christ. Nor did his devotion to the service of Christ prove the slightest obstacle to his professional success.

Although, as we have already seen, his pious father detected in him the incipient manifestations of a work of grace even in youth, yet it was not till he had reached full maturity that he made a public profession of his faith in Christ. This delay was doubtless because of his characteristic distrust of himself; for he was always a regular attendant upon the means of grace, and a liberal supporter of the institutions of religion. With the same zeal and whole-heartedness he devoted himself to his religious duties that he did to his temporal pursuits. He mastered that most difficult of all lessons in practical Christianity, to "use the world as not abusing it," —to keep it in its proper place of subordination. He made his daily life a service to the Lord. No offer, however tempting, could induce him to undertake a cause that had not justice upon its side. He had not a professional and a Christian conscience, the one to regulate his conduct at the bar, and the other in the Church of God. What he was upon the Sabbath, that he was during the whole week. The Word of God was the rule of his life. Christ was his Master, and in all things he endeavored to serve Him. This was doubtless the grand reason of his success.

He would have been a very poor advocate where his feelings were not enlisted, and poorer still if he had to argue against his own convictions. It was an easy matter when he was convinced that he was right, to convince others of the justice of his cause. But his character was so transparent that it would have been impossible for him to have concealed a fraud. He spoke from the heart, and his heart was overflowing with love for the wretched and sinful, because it had been penetrated by the love of Him who, when upon earth, was known as "the friend of publicans and sinners." Thus he succeeded in carrying into his professional life his Christian profession, keeping it pure and unsullied, and at the same time maintained, even to the last, his confidence in human nature, although he had, in the discharge of his duty, to become so conversant with the darkest phases of our poor, fallen, sinful humanity.

Very soon after connecting himself with the Presbyterian Church of Wyoming, where he first took the vows of God upon him, he was elected to its eldership. In a great measure the past and present prosperity of that church was due to his untiring efforts. When his residence was transferred to this city, some twelve years ago, although he would have received a warm welcome to any of our churches, he looked around, not to see where he would be most honored, and find the most congenial society, but where he could be most useful, and identified himself with Calvary Church, which was then, amid many discouragements, striving to maintain an existence. This inspired the little band of brethren here with confidence and courage. He was invited to his place in the eldership, and with untiring energy, devoting not only his time but also his means, he labored for its prosperity. If he was ever discouraged, he always succeeded in concealing his feelings. Always hopeful, always confident, he saw only the bright side. Nothing was ever permitted to interfere with his religious duties. It was a delight to him to lay aside his business cares and come to the house of prayer. His diligence in business did not abate the fervency of his spirit.

How often have we heard him plead with God, his voice tremulous with deepest emotion, for blessings upon this church and this city. He knew how to draw near to God. How earnest were his exhortations welling up from the very depths of his heart. This was very marked since his return from Europe, a little more than two years ago. The months which he spent there was the only season of relaxation he had given himself during his whole life. He was joyous as a child, while passing through the varied scenes of interest in the great theatre of the past. His was a nature to more than realize its anticipations. His sojourn in the old world was to him a long and delightful holiday; but we know its sad termination.

With his beloved wife he joined their only daughter and her husband in Europe, that together they might behold the things which were so familiar to them from extensive reading. The whole family were together, and their cup of happiness was full. But they were to learn how closely sorrow treads upon our present joys. Surrounded by the sublime and beautiful in nature, where they had selected a residence for some months, an infant grandson was placed in his aged arms. To one who had such great love for children this was happiness indeed. But the bud of promise drooped and died. Just before its departure, with his own hand he sprinkled upon it the symbolical water in the name of the sacred Three. Love and sorrow had alike consecrated him for this holy office.

But this was only the first step in a deeper baptism of sorrow. The young mother, the only child and daughter upon whom the wealth of affection of three loving hearts was lavished, had to follow her little one into the far-off country. At the moment of her departure he was with her and seemed to enter also within the gate. But she passed on alone. The glory for him faded away for a little. He only knew how near he had been to heaven by looking upon the face of his beloved dead, which continued illuminated by the rapture of the departing spirit. The influence of this scene he carried with him to the close of his life.

When he spoke of the vanity of earth and of the glory to be revealed, it was as Paul the aged spake after he had been transported to the third heavens. Eternal things were to him such realities. We expected to meet him a crushed and broken-hearted old man. But instead of this there was a saintly sweetness of patient resignation surrounding him, which increased as he ripened for heaven. The one great link which bound him to the future—for it is true that in old age parents live for their children rather than for themselves—severed, he did not cease from his labors, but abounded in them more and more, as if in haste to have his work done, that he might go home. The interests of the Church absorbed him more and more. His heart's desire and prayer to God was that the dissevered branches of our beloved Presbyterian Church might be reunited. For this he labored as well as prayed. I saw the tears of joy in his eyes when this union was at last consummated, and the two Assemblies brought together to ratify it.

But while he loved the whole Church and Christians of every name, it was upon this Church, which he served so faithfully as a ruling elder, that his heart's best affections were supremely fixed. Nothing could keep him from her solemn assemblies, not even the waning vigor of his powers.

Many of you will remember how, with tottering steps, he passed up the aisle, when for the last time he distributed the sacramental emblems. A less devoted man would have excused himself from duty. But the fervency of his spirit supplied the lack of physical vigor.

Well do I remember his last appearance in yonder pew. The text of the discourse was, "I am not alone, for the Father is with me." This was the promise upon which he was to lean ; the truth of which he was soon to test, and have fulfilled in his own experience. Little did we think as we saw him with slow and hesitating step, as if he would linger a little longer, leaving the house of God, and watched him beyond its sacred portals, that he was to pass them no more. But this was the will of God and we must bow in submission, although our loss is so great. "The Lord gave and the Lord hath taken away ;" we bless and magnify His holy name for all that He made him by His grace, and for all that He enabled him to accomplish here. Upon that Sabbath his work was really finished, although the Lord spared him to his family

for a few weeks longer, that they might lavish upon him the
tender ministrations of love.

We have to record the loving kindness and tender mercy
of our God to His servant. Goodness and mercy followed
him all the days of his life. He had served God in his generation, and by his life of active usefulness had testified to
the purifying and elevating power of divine grace. Nothing
could have added to the lustre of this testimony. It needed
not for its completion the raptures which God sometimes
vouchsafes to His servants in the hour of death. We needed
not the assurance from his lips that all was well with him.
And so we sought it not. Just as the sun, when it has run its
circuit through the heavens, gently sinks to rest behind the
gates of the west, and is lost to our sight, so did he pass
away. He had finished his course, and the Lord let fall upon
His departing servant the mantle of unconsciousness. There
was no pain, no fainting, no sickness, no languor. He "fell
on sleep" like the aged king of Israel who was the man after
God's own heart. When his work was done, the Master
sweetly whispered in his ear, "Rest from thy labor," and gave
"his beloved sleep."

The dear ones who watched so tenderly over him in his
last hours felt that he might awake at any moment. And he
did. Jesus came and awoke him out of his sleep. But who
can describe that awaking? Oh! did we know more of what
transpires between the dying saint and his Saviour, what a
scene could we present. He was ALONE, though his loving
wife and friends were ever near him. The hand of affection
which clasped his could feel no returning pressure. But think
you he was *alone?* Think you that the soul was wrap-
ped in the same unconsciousness as the body? I looked at
the lips from which words of mortal language would never
more pass, and I thought if it were lawful for him to
speak to us again, what wonders he could now reveal. And

yet I knew that from the depths of the dark valley where he then was, his soul was saying in rapture, "I fear no evil, for Thou art with me. Thy rod and Thy staff they comfort me."

The night was growing dark and tempestuous as for the last time I left his sacred chamber—sacred because it was the gate of heaven to an immortal soul. The midnight hour drew near. Sleep had forsaken my couch. A strange presence seemed to enter my chamber. No form did I see. No words did I hear. And yet it seemed as if he had tarried a moment on his ascending way, to say farewell, and leave the parting message he could not speak. It was as if I heard his familiar voice saying, "Farewell earth, with its dark, tempestuous nights. There is now no night for me. The light of unending day dawns upon me. I am rising above the clouds. Already do I realize the presence of my God and Saviour. Already do I see the loved ones for whom I mourned coming to meet me. Farewell! for I must away. Tell the dear ones whom my departure has left so desolate not to mourn. A little while, and our family divided in that foreign land shall be reunited in the Fatherland which I am now entering. Farewell! Farewell!"

I only speak for him. Comfort ye then one another with these his last words.

But, dear brethren and friends, let us lay to heart the great lesson of his life. We too can be "diligent in business; fervent in spirit; serving the Lord." Let us follow him so far as he followed Christ. Then life's duties done, death will be to us just what it has been to him—falling asleep in the arms of Jesus, to awake in His likeness, amid all the joys and blessed companionship of Heaven.

MEMORIALS AND RESOLUTIONS.

MEMORIAL OF THE SESSION OF CALVARY CHURCH.

A joint meeting of the Session, Deacons and Trustees of Calvary Church was held in the Chapel, Wednesday evening, June 7, 1871, for the purpose of giving expression to the feelings of the officers of this Church and congregation, in view of the great loss they have sustained in the death of Hon. John B. Skinner, who for several years was an Elder and Trustee of this Church and Society.

Rev. A. McLean was called to the chair. Geo. P. Putnam, Esq., was appointed secretary.

The following memorial was unanimously adopted :

On the sixth day of June, 1871, at eleven o'clock and twenty minutes P. M., our dear and venerated friend, Hon. John B. Skinner, parted from this mortal life, and entered, as we devoutly trust, upon the blessedness of the life eternal.

His relations to this Church from its organization, as an Elder, as President of its Board of Trustees, and as one of its most earnest and devoted members, have been so intimate, so pleasant, and to us so fraught with highest profit, that words can but feebly express our sense of bereavement.

When we remember, however, the long life which he was permitted to spend in that service which he loved, the ripeness of his
Christian experience, and the gentle hand that has led him in perfect
trust and peace to the " silent shore," our gratitude almost exceeds
our grief, and we bow in humble submission and thanksgiving.

Resolved, That this memorial be entered by the Clerk of Session
and by the Clerk of the Board of Trustees in their respective
minutes.

ACTION OF THE BAR OF ERIE COUNTY.

Pursuant to call, a meeting of the Bar of Erie County was
held at the Old Court House, yesterday afternoon, at five
o'clock. The attendance was quite large and a number of
distinguished jurists were among those present. The Hon.
Judge Verplanck called the assemblage to order and stated
the object of the meeting to be to take action in reference
to the death of the Hon. John B. Skinner. Upon his
motion, Hon. Millard Fillmore was called to preside, and
upon taking his chair asked the pleasure of the meeting.

On motion of Wm. H. Greene, Esq., Judge D. H. Bull,
of Cattaraugus county, and Hon. H. S. Cutting, were appointed secretaries. The organization being complete, the
following remarks were made from the chair :

REMARKS BY THE HON. MR. FILLMORE.

I am not in the habit of apologizing, but it has been so long
since I have attempted to speak in public that I fancy that I
feel somewhat like the aged prisoner released from the Bastile.
He had been confined so long that he had lost the use of his
limbs, and consequently his steps were hesitating and unsteady.
But feeble and unsatisfactory as my effort to speak may be, yet
I can not withhold my tribute of respect to the man whose death
we deplore to-day. I am not prepared to pronounce any eulogy

upon the character of Judge Skinner. Whoever shall assume that responsible duty will require time for reflection and preparation. But since I consented to-day to attend this meeting I have been too much occupied by previous engagements to find time even to read the brief obituary of the deceased published in the papers this morning. I shall therefore content myself by speaking of the Judge as I knew him. Doubtless there are many in this intelligent audience who knew him more intimately, if not so long as I have. My acquaintance commenced with him in 1829, when he and I were both members of the Assembly. That was my first year, but I think it was his third year, and he had then an enviable reputation for so young a man in that distinguished body, as yet free from the suspicion of bribery, and adorned by the talents of such men as John C. Spencer, Erastus Root, Benjamin F. Butler, Frank Granger, and a host of others. The revision of our statutes—the great work which did so much to methodize our laws and relieve them from the cumbrous language and accumulated contradictions and inconsistencies of years—was then just completed, and in that great work Judge Skinner bore a conspicuous part. I know that he was listened to with confidence and respect, and no member of the House seemed to exert a more salutary influence. But that, I believe, was his last year in the State Legislature, and party politics—not want of talent or integrity—prevented him from being elected to any popular office ; and, indeed, so long as I took part in party politics, we belonged to different parties, consequently my subsequent acquaintance was mainly at the bar. But here he was distinguished for his legal acquirements and forensic eloquence. I have often felt a tremor of anxiety when I had to meet him. He was a man religiously devoted to the interest of his client without ever compromising his own conscience or dignity. He prepared his case with great labor and assiduity, and whatever could be honorably said in favor of his client's interest he presented with great clearness and force, and when that was done he conceived he had discharged his professional duty, and he patiently awaited the result. But professional labors, however great and however successful, give but a limited reputation compared with official services. The reputation of the lawyer is confined mostly to the bench and bar, while that of the statesman or military hero fills the nation—and is often reflected from foreign countries. But the highest encomium which can ever be passed upon a man of his profession may with great propriety be passed upon him, and that is, he was a learned, conscientious lawyer.

"A wit 's a feather, and a chief 's a rod,
But an honest man is the noblest work of God."

As a citizen, his character stands without blemish. Foremost in all efforts to relieve the wants and improve the morals of society, he taught temperance rather by practice than by lectures; he adorned the Christian character by an humble, pious devotion, and was content to worship his Creator in his own way, without bigotry and free from all intolerance. Death is the common lot of humanity. It must come to us all sooner or later, and it can never touch a near and dear friend without our feeling it most sensibly. But yet there is some consolation in the thought that he was taken from us after his work was fully done. Had he died earlier, we should have felt that he and society had lost much. Had he survived the loss of health and faculties, we should have felt that his life was but prolonged misery, with no adequate compensation to himself or others. Our Creator knows best when it is time for us to die, and while we cannot avoid the pang which the death of a friend inflicts, yet it is our duty humbly to submit to the will of God and be resigned—and I feel that we but honor ourselves in honoring his memory.

S. S. Rogers, Esq., moved that a committee of five be appointed to draft resolutions expressive of the sense of the meeting; and the motion being adopted, the chair appointed as such committee the following gentlemen: S. S. Rogers, Esq., Judge Hall, Judge Daniels, E. G. Lapham, Esq., of Ontario, and George F. Danforth, Esq., of Monroe.

In the absence of the committee, the Hon. Judge Comstock, of Canandaigua, arose and paid a beautiful tribute to the memory of the deceased. He had known Judge Skinner in Wyoming county for fifteen years; and where he was best known as a lawyer, a Christian and a citizen, he stood preeminent. "As a lawyer," he said, "we all knew him; as an advocate he had few equals and no superior, and carried with him a force and fire which I never knew in any other man." He said that he made his client's case his own and threw the whole force of his strong nature into his cause. As a citizen he was without a stain upon his character. He was a man of fine culture, of excellent taste ; a genial, warm-hearted, sympathetic man, beloved by all, rich and poor alike. He had met him often at the Bar, and never had met his equal before a jury—never one who had exhibited more electrical power or displayed more convincing eloquence. He was a gentleman as well as a lawyer ; and while he never lowered his dignity, he never asserted any superiority to the discomfort or humiliation of others. Always kind to the younger members of the Bar, he was regarded by them in return with the warmest favor. For himself, he had always regarded Judge Skinner with feelings of admiration and love.

Mr. Rogers, from the committee on resolutions, submitted the following :

Resolved, That in the death of the Hon. John B. Skinner, the Bar of Western New York has lost one of its most honored and distinguished members, and the State a citizen of the highest character, purest morals and the most illustrious example.

For more than a generation he was a leader at our Bar worthy of the name. Able, eloquent, courageous, earnest, incorruptible, he adorned the profession which honored him. He loved that profession with no ignoble or mercenary passion. To him its members were ministers of justice, holding their offices and discharging their duties under the immediate supervision of the Great Judge ; and through an active and successful professional career, as well as through the years of a serene and peaceful age, he was known by all as a Christian gentleman.

Resolved, That a copy of these resolutions be presented at the General Term of the Supreme Court, now in session for the Fourth Judicial Department, and that the Secretary also furnish a copy thereof to the family of our venerated friend and brother, and that we will attend the funeral in a body.

Mr. Greene moved the adoption of the resolutions, and the motion was seconded.

T. B. Corlett, Esq., addressed the meeting briefly, in a strain of tender regard for the memory of the deceased.

Hon. R. P. Marvin, Judge of the Supreme Court, was the next gentleman to address the meeting. He said his acquaintance with Judge Skinner was of long standing, dating back thirty-nine or forty years in October. He first met him in the Court of Common Pleas, in Cattaraugus county; a Court which transacted most of the business that arose. He had at that time an established reputation as a lawyer. He had met him when the county was new—before the primeval forest had been disturbed—and the friendship he had formed with him then had continued without interruption down to the day of his death. He dated his first intimate acquaintance with Judge Skinner to the time when litigation arose in the county of an extraordinary character, and which extended into Pennsylvania. In this Judge Skinner took an active and important part. He complimented Judge Comstock's characterization of the man, and added that when he (the speaker) was placed upon the bench, Judge Skinner was in full practice. He said he was known for his intimate acquaintance with the nature of actions. He had never met a man who displayed such wonderful discrimination in regard to his actions. He knew when his action was complete and when his adversary's was faulty; and when he resisted a motion for a nonsuit it was because he was not to be nonsuited, while his demand for a nonsuit was invariably damaging to his adversary. The speaker said he was the most cautious man he ever knew in his preparation of a case, and informed himself of all its bearings; he was the most cautious man he ever knew in the trial of a cause; he followed his evidence step by step, and if the statement of an opposing witness crossed his theory, on the cross-examination he fairly exhausted his ingenuity to destroy or qualify it. He disposed summarily of a witness who did not affect him seriously. Few men were better in repartee;

but when the case went to the jury his highest powers were called into play. At that time, cases taken up on exceptions were rarely heard of, and the great merit was to get the cause before a jury. He said he thought he had never heard a man so powerful before a jury, and he confessed that after listening to one of his arguments he could not well see how a jury could do otherwise than render in his favor. Of all his earnestness, his severity, his playfulness, his power to command the sympathies of those whom he addressed—in a word, of his abilities as a true, great advocate, Judge Marvin spoke with eloquent simplicity and force. In denunciation and anathema he was terrible, but he was even more powerful when he appealed to a jury. At such time, his voice would sink down into a whisper, and would continue so for several minutes till his listeners were fairly enthralled. He had no quality of envy in his composition, and upon this point Judge Marvin dwelt with nicest delicacy. He concluded a beautiful tribute, which we have but merely outlined, by holding up the life of Judge Skinner as one worthy the emulation of the younger gentlemen of the Bar, and as a noble example for all.

Sherman S. Rogers, Esq., spoke from the standpoint of a ten years' friendship, formed after Judge Skinner's removal to Buffalo, since which time he had been substantially withdrawn from active professional life. He was not, therefore, to the speaker the eloquent advocate, the distinguished lawyer, but a friend who, though many years his senior, was as near and dear to him as if he were a kinsman of no remote degree.

He had nothing of assumption in his character; nothing to proclaim his greatness but the unmistakable qualities that belong to greatness. He was simple as a child, and readily formed attachments to young men. Upon coming to Buffalo he entered into our social life with activity and zest, and was esteemed and beloved by all. Age is winter to most men— a dark and cold and dreary season; but it was not so to

Judge Skinner. He trod the descending years of life in summer only.

Although so many years engaged in the practice of a profession which brought him into intimate acquaintance with the weakness and wickedness of men, he never lost his confidence in mankind, and never judged harshly or uncharitably.

He did not at any time forecast the future in gloom, but in serene and cheerful hope; a hope founded in that unwavering Christain faith which animated and enriched his whole life. It is only six months since he expressed to the speaker his conviction that he was becoming an old man. Before that he seemed as young in his feelings as any of us. Up to the time of his last illness he attended the meetings of all the societies of which he was a member; and through his illness there was always a cheerfulness in his manner and speech, and never a suggestion of gloom or discomfort.

He devoted his later years, after a brilliant professional career, to works of charity and philanthropy,—a beautiful close to a noble life.

Judge Hall very briefly addressed the meeting, and expressed his hearty concurrence in the words of eulogy which had fallen from the gentleman who had spoken. He said it was nearly, if not quite, forty years since, and in the same room, that he first met Judge Skinner; and that he well remembered that his distinguished learning, eloquence and ability was, even then, cheerfully acknowledged by those who were familiar with Judge Skinner's forensic efforts; that from that time he had been no stranger to Judge Skinner's high character and enviable reputation, and had since been associated with him in different relations; and that his more intimate personal intercourse with Judge Skinner enabled him to bear willing testimony to the purity of his life and the excellence of his example. That he was perfectly honest and upright, was active and earnest in all benevolent and useful enterprises, and generous and noble in his sympathies, purposes and conduct : that he was an honor to our common humanity and to the legal profession ; and that the profession most honored themselves in rendering the highest honors to his memory.

Hon. James O. Putnam paid his tribute of respect to the memory of the deceased in appropriate terms. He stated that his earliest associations were connected with Judge Skinner. He felt that he had sustained a personal loss in his death. The deceased was a man of most tender sensibilities and generous appreciation. He hated wrong and tyranny. For forty years he devoted himself to the most arduous duties of his profession, and in the closing years of his life he identified himself with public institutions directed to great good. He gave the last ten years of his life to the public. His character was truly worthy of imitation, as had been remarked. The latter portion of his life among us was a fitting close of a beautiful career.

After a few remarks by Mr. O. Olney, of Nunda, the resolutions were unanimously adopted, and the meeting adjourned.

THE BUFFALO GENERAL HOSPITAL.

At a recent meeting of the Board of Trustees of the Buffalo General Hospital, the following resolutions were passed :

Resolved, That in the death of the Hon. John B. Skinner, the Board of Trustees of the Buffalo General Hospital has lost a faithful and efficient presiding officer; the Hospital—an active, earnest and generous friend; and that this Board unites with the community, at large, in mourning the loss of a man whose life was devoted, for many years, to the discharge of the duties and occupations of the noble philanthropist and Christian gentleman.

Resolved, That this Board would respectfully tender to the widow of Mr. Skinner, its heartfelt sympathies in her bereavement, and would hereby direct the Secretary to enter these resolutions in the minutes of the proceedings of the Board and send a copy to Mrs. Skinner.

WM. F. MILLER,
Secretary.

BUFFALO AND ERIE COUNTY BIBLE SOCIETY.

At a meeting of the Buffalo and Erie County Bible Society, held June 20th, 1871, the following resolutions were submitted and, on motion, unanimously adopted:

Whereas, It has pleased God to remove from his sphere of usefulness in this world, to a sure reward in heaven, our lamented President, the Hon. John B. Skinner; therefore,

Resolved, That we hereby extend our condolence and sympathy to his afflicted widow and the relatives. Our Board feel that we have parted with a zealous friend and a wise counsellor in the cause of Bible distribution in this city and county. We sincerely deplore his loss as a public and private calamity, and for his many Christian virtues he will be cherished by us as a model worthy of emulation.

Resolved, That this memorial be recorded in our minutes, and that a copy be furnished to the widow of our deceased brother, and also for publication in our daily papers.

SILAS KINGSLEY,
Chairman.
JULIUS WALKER,
Secretary.

[*Extract from Secretary's Report at the Annual Meeting.*]
SECRETARY'S REPORT.

Mr. PRESIDENT:—The last annual meeting of our society was held on the 19th of June, 1870, and the business meeting on the Monday following, when the present board of officers were chosen.

I say present, but we have to make the exception of our lamented President, the Hon. John B. Skinner, who departed this life in the spring of 1871.

At a meeting of the Board held soon after, suitable resolutions of respect were passed and recorded in our minutes. It is due to the memory of the deceased, in this connection, that we should accord to him the tribute of having been a faithful servant. His relations to our Board were pleasant, and he won our confidence by his uniform Christian courtesy. We have felt the loss of his presence and counsel in giving direction and efficiency to the work of our society.

The memory of such a life and example will continue to exert a salutary Christian influence on the living, and is worthy of our emulation.

BUFFALO SAVINGS BANK.

At a special meeting of the Trustees of the Buffalo Savings Bank, held yesterday, the following resolutions were unanimously adopted :

Resolved, That this Board has learned, with deep regret and unfeigned sorrow, the decease of their late associate, the Hon. John B. Skinner.

Resolved, That in the death of Judge Skinner, this Board has lost an able adviser, a Trustee of large experience and sound judgment, conscientiously attentive to his duties, and ever ready to devote his time and talents to the promotion of the best interests of this institution.

Resolved, That, as individuals, we are deeply sensible of the loss we have sustained. We shall miss our venerable colleague, not only in our councils, but in social and personal intercourse, where his genial and kindly nature shone conspicuous, and where he exhibited those rare qualities and Christian graces, which not only won our admiration, but warmly attached us to his manly and noble character.

Resolved, That we tender to the family of the deceased our heartfelt sympathy and condolence for the loss they have sustained, and that we will, as a body, attend the funeral ceremonies.

Resolved, That the Secretary transmit a copy of these resolutions to the family of the deceased.

BUFFALO FEMALE ACADEMY.

Resolutions passed by the Board of Trustees of Buffalo Female Academy, June 15th, 1871 :

Resolved, That in the recent decease of Hon. John B. Skinner this Board has lost one of its most esteemed and useful members ; the friends of science and education, a most earnest and efficient co-worker ; and society a most useful citizen, who illustrated and honored his Christian profession by the purity of his life and the excellence of his example.

Resolved, That a copy of the above resolution be certified by the Secretary, and transmitted to the family of the deceased.

(A true copy from the records of the Board of Trustees of Buffalo Female Academy.)

A. T. CHESTER,
Secretary.

INGHAM UNIVERSITY, LE ROY.

The Committee appointed to draft a suitable memorial on the death of Hon. John B. Skinner reported as follows :

It having pleased our Heavenly Father to remove by death from his earthly labors our late highly esteemed associate, Hon. John B. Skinner, of Buffalo, we deem it fitting to make the following minute of the sense of the Council in relation to this sad bereavement.

Resolved, 1. That we are hereby solemnly impressed with the brevity and uncertainty of life, and reminded that we live even in the shadow of the tomb.

2. That we gratefully recognise and cherish the memory of the personal worth of our departed fellow-laborer and the great value of his services in the cause of Christian education.

3. That while we address ourselves to the part assigned us in the work of life, we accept the lesson conveyed by this dispensation, to do with renewed diligence and zeal what our hands find to do for Christ and His Church, and the rising generation.

4. That this minute go on the records of Ingham University, and a copy of the same be transmitted to the family of the deceased.

C. H. TAYLOR,

Secretary.

NEW YORK STATE INSTITUTION FOR THE BLIND, AT BATAVIA.

BATAVIA, June 14th, 1871.

At a meeting of the Board of the Trustees of this Institution, held as above, the death of the Hon. John B. Skinner, our late President, having been announced, the following resolutions were adopted :

Resolved, That by the decease of the Hon. John B. Skinner, late President of this Board, the Trustees have lost a valued associate and able counsellor ; the Institution a warm and devoted friend, and the cause of virtue and education, one of its most efficient advocates and promoters.

Resolved, That the Secretary of this Board transmit a copy of these resolutions to the family of the deceased.

R. BALLARD,

Secretary.

MEMORIAL OF THE PRESBYTERIAN CHURCH AT WYOMING, NEW YORK.

The Session of the Presbyterian Church of Wyoming, N. Y., at its first meeting after the death of Hon. John B. Skinner, of Buffalo, adopted the following memorial :

In this place Judge Skinner spent the greater part of his active life. Here he professed the Christian faith and became one of the active, efficient and devoted members of this Church. For many years he was a member of this Session, and we bear loving and willing testimony to the faithfulness with which he discharged his private and his official duties.

Where two or three were gathered for prayer he was one, and the tenderness and warmth of his devotions were an inspiration to others -- now they are a pleasing and blessed memory.

When difficulties were to be removed, he was wise in council and efficient in action. Liberal in his contributions, he ministered to the wants of the Church of which he was an overseer, and was deeply interested in the various fields of Christian benevolence, and although more than ten years have passed since his immediate connection with this Church terminated by his removal to another field of labor, he continued to manifest a deep interest in our welfare while he lived.

Having known Judge Skinner long and well, it is our duty and pleasure to bear testimony to the excellence of his Christian character and example. Dignified, yet courteous and affable, his presence was always a restraint upon immorality and vice, thus exerting a most salutary influence upon his associates in business and society.

His early, laborious and persistent efforts in behalf of temperance deserve to be distinctly and gratefully acknowledged.

As a Session and as a Church we deeply sympathize with his bereaved family in our common loss.

We trust that this Providence may lead us all to consecrate ourselves more fully to the service of Him who "doeth all things well," and to whom we should look for support in all our weakness and woe.

HUGH T. BROOKS,
O. G. KEITH,
Committee.

At a meeting of the Session of the Presbyterian Church of Wyoming, held Feb. 26, 1862 (soon after Mr. S. removed to Buffalo), the following minute was unanimously adopted :

The Session of the Presbyterian Church of Wyoming in parting from the Hon. J. B. Skinner, with whom for many years they have been so pleasantly associated, feel constrained to express the deep regret with which they comply with his request for a letter of dismission.

They delight to bear testimony to the readiness with which, at all times, he gave to the service of the Church his eminent abilities, his means and his influence. They rejoice that the good providence of God yet spares him to continue his usefulness elsewhere, and would assure him that their affection and high regard shall be in no wise diminished by this painful separation of a relation so intimate and so long enduring.

By order of Session,

J. JONES,

Moderator.

EXTRACTS FROM THE PAPERS.

OBITUARY—HON. JOHN B. SKINNER.

Another of our venerable citizens has gone to his final home. Although the sad event has been expected for some time, the announcement that our venerable fellow-townsman, Judge Skinner, is no more, will be received with sharp sorrow by a vast number of the people of Buffalo and Western New York, and, indeed, by people throughout the State and nation.

John B. Skinner, son of Benjamin Skinner, of Williamstown, Berkshire county, Mass., was born July 23d, 1799, in a house erected by Col. Simonds, his maternal grandfather, on the bank of the Hoosack river. His paternal grandfather was the Rev. Thomas Skinner, a graduate of Harvard University, and during his whole ministerial life, pastor of the Congregational church at Westchester, Conn. His father was one of the first settlers of Williamstown; assisted in the erection of Williams College, and was ever liberal and efficient in support of the interests of the Church and every Christian and benevolent enterprise. John B. graduated from Williams in 1818; read law with the Hon. David Buel, of Troy, and after attending a course of lectures at the law school of Judges Reeves and Gould, at Litchfield,

Conn., we understand that he spent some time in Gov. Marcy's office, but whether before or after his admission to the Bar, we do not learn. Between young Skinner and the Governor there existed a warm friendship which only terminated with the death of the latter. He was admitted to the Supreme Court of the State of New York in August, 1821. His advantages were of the highest order ; the young student knew how to use them for what they were worth; and with a thorough knowledge of his profession, high aspirations and a determination to succeed, he entered upon his career as a lawyer. He commenced practice in the town of Middlebury, near the centre of the old county of Genesee, at present known as the village of Wyoming, in the county of the same name—both named by him.

His thorough knowledge of the law, his indefatigable industry, his enthusiasm and eloquence, and genial manners soon attracted attention, and business flowed in upon him from the neighboring counties, which continued and increased until he retired from the practice. In the year 1826, when the two political parties were under the great leaders De Witt Clinton and Martin Van Buren, without his solicitation he was nominated for the Assembly, and although the opposing party had been in the ascendancy for years, he was elected by an overwhelming majority. He was re-elected the two succeeding years, without opposition, a compliment which had never before, and has never since, been paid to any individual in the district. As a member of the Legislature, he was among the most prominent. He was Chairman of the Committee upon Literature and of many important select committees ; and the Journals of the House and the political history of the period supply ample evidence as to how admirably he discharged his duties. In the year 1838, he was, at the solicitation of the Bar, nominated by Gov. Marcy and unanimously confirmed by the Senate, Circuit Judge and Vice Chancellor of the Eighth District. In 1846, he was appointed District Judge of the Court of Common Pleas, which office he held until the change of the Constitution abolished the office. In 1852, he was, with the Hon. Horatio Seymour, appointed State delegate to the Baltimore Convention, which nominated Gen. Pierce for President; and the next year one of the Presidential Electors to cast for him the vote of the State. In 1853, he was appointed Attorney of the United States for the Northern District of New York, an office of much responsibility and greatly sought for, but which, owing to his business in the State Courts, he respectfully declined.

In 1830, Mr. Skinner was married to Catharine, only daughter of Richard M. Stoddard, one of the most prominent of the early settlers of Western New York. This amiable and accomplished lady died in 1833. He was again married in 1837 to Sarah A., daughter of Henry G. Walker, of Wyoming, who bore him one daughter, his only child, the late Mrs. Josiah Letchworth.

At an early period of his residence at Wyoming, Judge Skinner united with the Presbyterian Church, of which he was soon appointed an elder, and his liberal and active efforts contributed much to raise this Church from a feeble beginning to a position of influence in that community. He identified himself with the moral and religious progress of an active and earnest people, and at the time of his removal from the county was President of the Bible, Temperance and Colonization Societies ; and it may be truly said of him that few men have been more widely known or have exerted a more salutary influence.

In the year 1860, he removed to this city, having previously secured one of the finest locations here ; and since that time he has enjoyed, in comparative retiracy, the fruits of an active and laborious life. At the time of his death he was a member of the Board of Education of the Presbyterian Church ;

President of the Board of Trustees of the New York State Asylum for the Blind, an institution recently established at Batavia, and one of the noblest charities of the age ; President of the State Normal School, in this city ; Vice-President of the Reformatory at Warsaw ; a member of the Board of Trustees of the Buffalo Female Academy, and also a member of the Board of Trustees of the Buffalo City Savings Bank.

His broad and active benevolence invited the manifold responsibilities of a charitable and humane order which pressed upon him ; and in the discharge of the duties incident to them he was gratifying his very highest ambition.

As an advocate, few men in the State enjoyed a higher reputation than Judge Skinner. The known purity and uprightness of his character, his comprehensive knowledge of men, his great readiness and self-command, combined with an earnest and impressive manner, enchained the attention while it enlisted the sympathies of a jury, and he very rarely failed to carry them with him. As a judge he was clear, quick in apprehension, and prompt in decision, and these characteristics rendered him useful, reliable and popular on the bench. Indeed, there were no qualities wanting in Judge Skinner to make him the consummate lawyer and the able jurist. His mind eminently fitted him for statesmanship, but he fairly shrank from public life, and whatever of political prominence he had, he owed first to an ardent devotion to the principles of the Democratic party, and secondly to an intense desire on the part of those who knew him to compel him to act in public life. Undoubtedly the most reasonable explanation of his avoidance of everything that could be interpreted to mean political ambition, was his great love for his profession and his undying attachment to persons, places and things. It is said of him, that if he owned an old horse it was to him the best horse in the world and worthy of his kindest and most thoughtful attentions, and he never wished to part with it.

The same constancy was expressed toward everything he loved, and such men out of their *habitat* are never truly themselves. He was a man of the very strongest convictions; and as a Democrat of the old school and a communicant in the Presbyterian Church, his faith was unqualified and unwavering. The religious element of his character was largely unfolded, and with an active and profound benevolence he was a thoroughly Christian gentleman. He was catholic and liberal in his views; was decidedly an optimist, and viewed human nature, with all its shortcomings, with the kindliest eyes; and his masculine will and power were so blended with exquisite tenderness as to present him as the incarnation of strength and delicacy. He has always been known for his fine sensibilities, and equally well for the irresistible power he exerted when arrayed against a bad man or a great wrong. Whenever he was compelled to apply the lash, he threw the whole strength of his nature into the business and was merciless; but no appeal to his heart was ever made in vain. Through the iron of his character ran a vein of silver, and he was known of men to be as truly good as he was nobly strong. In his later years he filled the term "venerable" to perfection, and the radiance of his pure and lofty life, his fidelity to principle, his genuine manliness, his large benevolence, and his loving and lovable nature, should keep his memory green forever. — *Buffalo Courier, June 8, 1871.*

OBITUARY—DEATH OF HON. JOHN B. SKINNER.

Another of our aged and best known citizens has made answer to the death summons. Tuesday evening, after a somewhat protracted illness, the Hon. John B. Skinner expired at his residence, No. 155 North street, closing an unusually busy and useful life of nearly seventy-two years. His career is honorably and prominently associated with the legal profession in Western New York. Offices of high respectability were entrusted to him, and he performed the duties pertaining to them with spotless integrity and marked ability. He was identified with almost every benevolent and educational public enterprise in this section of the State, devoting, in obedience to the sympathies of a generous heart, his time and money freely in aid of anything designed for the extension of charity to the poor and enlightenment to the masses. During the years of his life in Buffalo he held the respect and confidence of our people in the fullest degree, not wealth alone but excellences of character securing him high professional and social standing.—*Buffalo Express, June 8, 1871.*

OBITUARY—HON. JOHN B. SKINNER.

We, yesterday afternoon, in a brief article, gave publicity to the deeply-regretted fact of the death of the venerable Judge John B. Skinner, of this city. The demise of one so well known and highly esteemed in this community, and throughout the State, calls for more than a passing notice at our hands.

The deceased was born at the old homestead in Williamstown, Mass., July 23d, 1799, and was the son of Benjamin Skinner, Esq. His father was one of the earliest settlers of Williamstown and prominently identified with the foundation of Williams College. The late Judge was a graduate of Williams College, in the class of 1818. After graduating, he commenced the study of law in the office of Hon. David Buel, of Troy, and subsequently attended a course of lectures at Litchfield, Conn., where he had the sound teachings of Judges

Gould and Reeves. For some time he also studied in Gov. William L. Marcy's office, and the friendship engendered at that time was lasting and sincere. In the year 1821 the subject of this sketch was admitted to the Supreme Court of this State. He first entered upon practice in Middlebury, Genesee county, now known as Wyoming. His early career as a lawyer was attended with success, and his untiring industry and urbanity of disposition gave satisfaction to his clients and won the love of all who came in contact with him.

In 1826, he was nominated by Democratic constituents for the Assembly, and was elected by a large majority. This was at the time when the Clinton and Van Buren factions were earnestly opposing each other in this State. He was elected for the two succeeding terms, a deserved compliment and of which he justly felt proud. When in the Legislature he was Chairman of the Committee on Literature and other important select committees. In 1838, he was nominated by Gov. Marcy, at the solicitation of the Bar, as Circuit Judge and Vice-Chancellor of the Eighth District. His nomination was confirmed by the Senate. In 1846, he was appointed District Judge of the Court of Common Pleas, which office he held until the change of the Constitution abolished the office. In 1852, he was, with the Hon. Horatio Seymour, appointed State delegate to the Baltimore Convention, which nominated Franklin Pierce for President; and the next year one of the Presidential Electors to cast for him the vote of the State. In 1853, he was appointed Attorney of the United States for the Northern District of New York, an office of much responsibility, which, owing to his business in the State Courts, he declined to accept.

In 1830, Judge Skinner was married to Catharine, only daughter of Richard M. Stoddard, one of the early settlers of Western New York. This esteemed lady died in 1833. He was again married in 1837 to Sarah A., daughter of Henry

G. Walker, of Wyoming. Their only offspring was the late Mrs. Josiah Letchworth.

As a member of the Presbyterian Church, with which he identified himself as an earnest and able worker, his influence for good was great, and his loss is irreparable.

He came to Buffalo to live in 1860, and since that time had resided at the fine place on North street, well known as one of the most desirable locations in the city. At the time of his death he was a member of the Board of Education of the Presbyterian Church ; President of the Board of Trustees of the New York State Asylum for the Blind, an institution recently established at Batavia ; President of the State Normal School, in this city ; Vice-President of the Reformatory at Warsaw ; a member of the Board of Trustees of the Buffalo Female Academy, and also a member of the Board of Trustees of the Buffalo City Savings Bank. He was prominently identified with the Erie County Bible Association ; and in the positions of President of the Buffalo General Hospital, and one of the Board of Trustees of that institution, he exerted a great influence. He was faithful and efficient in the discharge of his duties in connection with this noble institution, and labored as long as he had strength. The Board of Trustees feel that his place cannot be filled. No one of our citizens has done more to increase the efficiency of the Hospital.

To properly eulogize a character so estimable as the lamented deceased would be a difficult task. Natures like his are like the sun, which sheds its radiance on all around. Such a life is of itself an example. Pure in his public and social intercourse, broad and liberal in his views of humanity, his daily walks were in the direction of the greatest good ; nor time nor occasion prevented him from using his influence where it was most needed. His mental acquirements were great, and despite the engrossing cares of duty, and the demand upon his time, his heart was always kind, and his sympathy gushed forth like a well spring when any direct appeal to his humanity was made. The young loved Judge Skinner, for he ever took a kindly interest in their welfare. Little deeds of goodness and expressions of solicitude from the aged to those of youthful years, take their place in memory's tenderest recollections, and endure with perennial freshness. So that not only those more nearly of the age of the late Judge revere and love his memory, but many of our city's youth deeply feel the loss of so good a man. He has gone to rest in the ripeness of age. Few die more worthy of the crown of the blessed. A pure spirit has ascended to meet the reward of a life well spent, full of good deeds and faithful to the end.

There will be a meeting of the members of the Bar of Erie County, at the General Term rooms, old Court House, this afternoon at five o'clock, to take action in reference to the decease of Hon. Jno. B. Skinner.—*Buffalo Commercial Advertiser, June 8, 1871.*

HON. J. B. SKINNER.

MESSRS. EDITORS,—Your last issue contains a brief but fitting notice of this eminent jurist and useful church officer. The writer well says that "he deserves more than a passing notice," and we anticipate the appearance of an "in memoriam discourse" from his pastor, Rev. Alexander McLean. His public life covered a period of great historic interest in Western New York, with the events of which he had much to do. A gentleman of cultivated mind, studious habits, legal acumen, courtesy of manner, flexibility of voice, and power to awaken emotion at his pleasure, his services were often secured in cases where the heart was to be moved as

well as the intellect informed. While these qualities made
him a man of power in the court room, they also contributed
to the commanding place he held in the religious meeting
and our ecclesiastical courts. My acquaintance with the
deceased went back a score of years, while my respect and
affection increased to the last, in common with multitudes
throughout this region.

The writer in the *Observer* speaks of Judge Skinner as
" holding several important positions at the time of his death
—as President, Trustee, Director, &c. ; " but there is another
which was to the deceased one of the most endearing of his
life—Trustee of Geneseo Academy. So soon as he learned
the religious character of this institution, the conversions
constantly occurring within its walls, the additions made
from its alumni to the ministry (home and foreign), the happiness it was sending to hearts and homes, he became a munifi-
cent donor to its treasury, a judicious counsellor and warm-
hearted advocate, wherever he could present its merits and
plead its claims. For all this, we of Western New York
remember him with grateful affection.   W.

—*New York Observer, June, 1871.*

THE LATE JUDGE SKINNER.

New York, June 19, 1871.

Editor Buffalo Commercial Advertiser,—An intimate acquaintance and friend of the late Hon. John B.
Skinner, I heard of his death a few days since with the most
painful emotions. I became acquainted with him in the year
1839, and have seen much of him, at times, since that period,
under circumstances of the most unreserved private friendship.

There are sentiments and feelings in this world too deep and too sacred for public utterance. Those that I entertain for my departed friend are of this character, and I shall not, therefore, attempt to express them, were it even otherwise proper to do so.

With regard to his public character the same reticence is not required, nor, in his case, whose character was in so many respects an exalted model for others, is it either expedient or desirable. His professional morality was of the most elevated as well as discriminating character. While this fact is conspicuously recognized by the several speakers at the recent meeting of the members of the Bar of Erie County, and also in the obituary notices that have been taken of him, there are some special exemplifications of this trait of his character which deserve special mention, not merely because they are creditable to him, but also because of the beneficial influence they will exert upon others, especially the younger members of the profession. It is well known to all his friends and acquaintances in Wyoming and adjoining counties, where his ordinary professional services were chiefly called into requisition, that it was his habitual custom, whenever called upon for advice and counsel, in all civil cases, to make a serious effort to bring about an amicable settlement, and this wholly without reference to any real or supposed advantages to accrue to himself by an opposite course. Especially was this true of his immediate neighbors. He was the true and unselfish friend of them all; preventing by his manly, Christian course much of that petty litigation which is so rife in some communities—many of those heartburnings and neighborhood jealousies which are too often, under similar circumstances, fostered and encouraged.

Early in his professional career he prescribed to himself the rule never to undertake a case as counsel for plaintiff unless his client had, in his estimation, after a full understanding of the matter, either law or equity on his side. It is doubtful whether he ever consciously departed in a single instance from this rule. The intensity of his personal attachments may at times have overpowered his judgment, but, if so, they were exceptional cases; so rare indeed that they proved the truth of the rule he laid down for himself. That he adhered scrupulously and religiously to the rule is well known, and that too under many circumstances immediately disadvantageous, pecuniarily, to himself. Such a course as this could not fail in the end to give him both influence and power in the community where he lived, and co-extensive with his professional engagements. His great influence with both court and jury was due primarily perhaps to his admitted legal abilities and acquirements; but secondarily certainly to the fact of his rigid adherence to the rule above indicated. His example in this respect is too valuable not to be considered, and it may safely be commended to universal imitation. Its public importance will, I trust, prove to the immediate relatives of the deceased a sufficient apology for this intrusion of an attached friend. W. L. B.

FROM A LETTER OF THE REV. R. H. NASSAU, MISSIONARY IN WESTERN AFRICA.

Of Judge Skinner's public life I know only as a stranger reads or hears. I do not think of him thus. I see him as he was in his home life.

Looking across the years and trying to bridge the miles of ocean between Africa and America, I have often rested, as on a beautiful picture, in the memory of a cherished acquaintance with Judge Skinner at home.

I remember that in the Spring and Summer of 1859, while on a visit to my brother, Rev. J. E. Nassau, at Warsaw, Judge

Skinner came from Wyoming as committee of the Church Session, to invite me to the Wyoming pulpit. The roads were very heavy with mud and the late Spring rain was cold. I recall his paternal care of me in the wrappings of the carriage he was driving. And not more warmly than this thoughtful care glowed the warm wood fire on the hospitable hearth of his pleasant home, when, during the few weeks in which I supplied the pulpit, I was admitted within the charmed precincts of his family circle.

His well-stored mind made association with him not simply a privilege but a positive pleasure. His books were his friends, and his conversation was not labored, or pedantic, or an offensive exhibition of acquisitions.

I was a young man, just graduate of the Theological Seminary; but he, covering by his courtesy the difference in our years, made me feel during those talks in his carriage, or in the parlor, on the veranda, or under the trees, as if both were recalling reminiscences of travel, or history, or character, or art, which we had each seen, known, or had a part in.

His taste gratified itself and those around him in his rural home, by gathering to it whatever was best and truly beautiful, not what was simply expensive or gaudy. While still a student at Princeton, riding one vacation through Wyoming, I had noticed the simple beauty and delicate taste of the grounds enclosing the house and office (both literally embowered in foliage), which, two years later, I learned to know as Judge Skinner's residence. He took almost a child's pleasure in watching the growth of his young trees, and in pointing out the arrangement of plants with reference to harmony of colors in the flower gardens.

I remember so distinctly his trying to straighten a bruised daisy among others planted on the border of a sunny slope, a favorite spot of his tenderly loved and accomplished daughter Mary, afterwards Mrs. J. Letchworth.

Now that they are both "under the daisies," I write these few lines at the promptings of an attached and grateful memory.

A few months ago, on revisiting Wyoming after twelve years' absence, I sought Judge Skinner's former residence. The spot of course I could not forget, but I hesitated for a moment as to the house. The Autumn winds had laid bare the trees—no little winding paths—no daisy borders. I knocked at the door, intending to ask if I might again enter the parlor that had once been so genial. There was no response, and I did not regret it, for the contrast would have left a painful memory. Passing down the gravelled walk and out the gate, I remembered that one beautiful summer night I had stood there with him, our thoughts led up to God and back again to earth. He was always sympathetic—I had never seen him sad : but now, in a voice tremulous with emotion, he asked why the beautiful on earth was so often sad. I rejoice for him that he has gone where all is beauty in perfection, and where sadness never comes.

R. H. NASSAU.

MEMORIAL PAPER

READ BEFORE THE BUFFALO HISTORICAL SOCIETY,
FEBRUARY 24, 1873, BY HON. JAMES O. PUTNAM.

Lawyers are said to have brief histories. So many early struggles, so many contests before courts and juries over questions of a narrow interest, and then an end. Unless called to important public positions, and thus his life becomes identified with large public interests, it is certainly true, the lawyer of the highest professional reputation leaves little material for the biographer. The life of Judge Skinner, eminent as it was in his chosen profession, offers no exception to this rule. His whole career, with the exception of a short experience in the State Legislature, while he was yet a young man, was of unsurpassed constancy to his profession. This devotion, however, was not at the expense of much public service, through his connection with religious, educational and charitable institutions, while his personal character for nearly half a century was a recognized power in the State. But because he was so eminent in his profession, I regret that the office of preparing the memorial paper for the Historical Society was not devolved upon some one who was intimately associated with his professional life, for I can speak only of his professional reputation. My embarrassment is somewhat relieved by the suggestion of the committee that I supplement my sketch from other intelligent and appreciative sources.

John B. Skinner was born in Williamstown, Massachusetts, July 23, 1799. His family represented the highest character and culture of New England. Col. Simonds, his maternal grandfather, was distinguished for his patriotic services in the war of the Revolution, and his honorable fame is one of the cherished local traditions of Berkshire. His paternal grandfather was the Reverend Thomas Skinner, who was educated at Harvard University, studied for the ministry, and was settled for life over the Congregational Church of Middleton, Connecticut. His father, Deacon Benjamin Skinner, was distinguished in his time for his devotion to religious and educational interests. He was one of the early friends of Williams College, where his sons were educated. His son, John B., graduated in 1818. After graduation he entered the law office of Hon. Daniel Ball, of Troy, N. Y., where he formed a life-long friendship with his fellow student, the late Governor Marcy. He completed his preparatory legal studies at the then celebrated law school of Judges Gould and Reeves, at Litchfield, Conn. He was admitted to the Supreme Court of the State, in August, 1821.

In about the year 1821 he sought the then land of promise, for New England enterprise and adventure, Western New York. Wyoming, in the town of Middlebury, county of Genesee, which he made his residence, was but a hamlet, with little promise, we should say, for a brilliant professional career. Yet, although large inducements were often presented him to remove to more ambitious social and business centres, he resisted every importunity to change his residence until his retirement from the practice of his profession. His success, solid and brilliant, was assured from the first. His industry, his fidelity to professional trusts, his learning and his marvelous power before juries, gave him a leadership at the circuits which he never lost. The jury trial was the favorite theatre of his professional contests, and it was as the advocate that he was without a peer. The methods of conducting litigation in his time differed from the present. Then the great object was to secure a verdict from the twelve men. On their decision hung the issues of life and death and fortune. This made the counsel who could carry the jury, whether by magic or storm, an indispensable ally. Appeals were comparatively rare. Now-a-days when the jury in so many trials is but an incident, and law, as has been said with much humor and some wisdom, is the power of decision by the last judge that can hear the case, the eloquent advocate holds a position less relatively important in the trial of causes. But Judge Skinner was learned as a lawyer, as well as eloquent as an advocate, and it was this rare combination that gave him a position so distinguished before the courts. This sketch would fail of a proper presentation of his professional character, if, as I have already suggested, I was unable to present the fair estimate of him by some of his professional cotemporaries and associates. At a meeting of the Bar of Erie County, convened to give some expression to its sentiment on the occasion of his death, were several appreciative addresses.

Ex-President Fillmore, in the course of his opening remarks as chairman of the meeting, said :

" My acquaintance commenced with Mr. Skinner in 1829, when he and I were both members of the Assembly. That was my first year, but I think it was his third year, and he had then an enviable reputation for so young a man in that distinguished body as yet free from the suspicion of bribery, and adorned by the talents of such men as John C. Spencer, Erastus Root, Benjamin F. Butler, Frank Granger, and of others. The revision of our statutes, the great work which did so much to methodise and relieve them from the cumbrous language and accumulated contradictions and inconsistencies of years, was then just completed, and in that great work Judge Skinner bore a conspicuous part. I know that he was listened to with confidence and respect, and no member of the House seemed to exert a more salutary influence. My subsequent acquaintance with him was mainly at the Bar. Here he was distinguished for his legal arguments and forensic eloquence. I have often felt a tremor of anxiety when I have had to meet him. He was a man religiously devoted to the interest of his client, without even compromising his own conscience or dignity. He prepared his case with great labor and assiduity, and whatever could be said in favor of his client's interest he presented with great clearness and force, and when that was done he conceived he had discharged his professional duty, and he patiently waited the result. The highest encomium that can ever be passed upon a man of his profession may with great propriety be passed upon him, and that is, he was a learned, conscientious lawyer."

From Hon. James R. Doolittle, late U. S. Senator, of Wisconsin, I have received the following note :

Mr. Putnam,—*Dear Sir :* The late John B. Skinner, as a lawyer and advocate, had few equals, and no superior for many years in Western New York. To uniform courtesy, untiring industry, unflinching and incorruptible fidelity to his clients, you must add great tact and knowledge of human nature, as well as great legal learning, and oftentimes the highest order of eloquence, to make a just estimate of his character. It was before a jury that in some respects he was unequalled. His efforts there were entirely extemporaneous. Those who have had great opportunity to hear the most eloquent of American orators, say there were occasions when these extemporaneous efforts of Mr. Skinner, in true eloquence and power, surpassed all his contemporaries. When fully roused his language was pure English, chaste, elegant and concise. He spoke without apparent effort, with a directness, earnestness and naturalness that seemed almost inspired. His mind, like his person, was high wrought and of the finest mould. All his appeals and all his conversations were addressed to the better part of our nature. With truth it may be said, no one ever heard him at the Bar, or held private conversation with him, who did not feel his nobler sentiments strengthened and elevated by his influence.

JAMES R. DOOLITTLE.

February 7, 1873.

The Hon. Martin Grover, Judge of the Court of Appeals, probably knew him more intimately in his professional character during the last twenty years of Mr. Skinner's practice at the Bar, than any other man now living. He has very kindly furnished a sketch which I have great pleasure in embodying in this paper :

In compliance with your request in behalf of the Buffalo Historical Society, that I should furnish some information in regard to the professional career of the late Judge Skinner, I will briefly do so.

I became acquainted with him in 1836. He then resided in Middlebury, Wyoming county, and had acquired a very large practice in his profession, his attention being principally devoted to the trial of cases at circuit. He attended all the circuits in Livingston, Allegany, Cattaraugus, Chautauqua and Genesee counties, and his presence was regarded almost as essential as that of the judge. There were then no railroads in any part of the district, and Judge Skinner traveled from one county town to another, in company with the judge, each with his own horse and sulky.

Extensive study and large experience had made Mr. Skinner perfectly familiar with and master of nearly every legal question presented, and he was therefore able to take a leading part in nearly every case tried. His clear intellect and capacity for quick comprehension enabled him to try a cause with great ability, without any previous preparation, and with but little consultation with his client or the other counsel. He would grasp the entire case at once and adopt the correct mode of conducting the trial. He was very sagacious in the examination of witnesses. An adverse witness rarely succeeded in baffling him, and as a general rule he would derive an advantage for his client from the reluctance of such a witness to disclose the whole truth. But his great power was in summing up to the jury. In this I have never seen one superior and scarcely ever his equal. His clear statements and close logical arguments usually convinced the understanding of his hearers, and when to these were added his powers of persuasion, the effect was overwhelming. He possessed in an eminent degree the highest powers of an orator. In listening to him no one could doubt his entire sincerity, and when he appealed to the highest and noblest principles of humanity it was the outpouring from the heart. His words went directly to the hearts of the audience. His control of their emotions was for the time complete. Nothing seemed to give him greater pleasure than the exertion of these high faculties in the cause of justice. He was a gentleman of the old school, and exhibited these traits in all his conduct during a trial. Always courteous to the Bench, though firm and earnest in insisting upon the rights of his client. His uniform politeness to the adverse party, counsel and witnesses, had a strong tendency to restrain undue exhibitions of passion, too frequently witnessed upon exciting trials.

The elegance of his style proved his correct literary taste and thorough scholarship. It is possible that my views of the qualities and powers of Judge Skinner may have been somewhat biased by my want of experience when I first became acquainted with him. That was at the commencement of my practice. I had then attended the trial of but few causes. Since then I have had the pleasure of hearing many of those most eminent in the different sections of the State, and while listening, have often mentally compared them with Judge Skinner.

I believe I am correct in saying that he was excelled by none in the highest qualities of oratory. His known high sense of honor and strict integrity added to the confidence reposed in him by jurors. They knew that he would scorn to misstate the law, or misrepresent the facts. His knowledge of poetry and the best English classics not only gave him polish of diction, but furnished facilities for happy illustration.

Owing to his residence being remote from the places where the appellate courts were held, he rarely appeared before these tribunals. Hence he has left in the reports no monuments of his forensic learning and skill. That he was regarded as a sound and able lawyer by those best qualified to judge, was evinced by his appointment as Circuit Judge, and *ex-officio* Vice-Chancellor in 1838, by that able jurist and eminent statesman, William L. Marcy, at that time Governor. This offer he declined, as he did others, preferring the practice of the profession. This he industriously pursued until admonished by the infirmity of age that he required rest. He then retired, having acquired a competency by legitimate earnings in the profession, and the last years of his life were solaced by literary pursuits and social intercourse with his early friends. His attachment to these was strong. His love for the law, as a science, continued after he retired from practice. Whenever I had the pleasure of passing much time in his company, that, with him, was a favorite subject of conversation.

He was a sound lawyer, a great orator, an accomplished gentleman and a devoted Christian. No one in Western New York has added more to the honor and dignity of its Bar. He has completed his works and passed away, leaving a noble example for his surviving associates.

M. GROVER.

ALBANY, February 7th, 1873.

The expressions of these distinguished gentlemen, who had the advantage of long personal and professional intimacy with Mr. Skinner, are doubtless a just estimate of him as a lawyer and advocate.

What might have been his success in the highest range of discussion, we can only imagine. He never had the opportunity which a great public cause and a great occasion afford to the orator. But when we remember the integrity of his mind, his keen sense of right and wrong, his intense convictions, and that sensibility and fervor which charged his utterance with a magnetism that was electric, we cannot doubt he would have taken high rank in any deliberative body. There can be no question as to the rank Judge Skinner held, not only in point of professional ability, but of professional character. He was of that class of lawyers who, in the best days of all civilized states, have made the legal profession the ally of religion and virtue in advancing the social and civic interests of mankind. His profession he accepted as a sacred trust. That trust was administered with a conscientiousness that reflects honor upon human nature.

Said a friend, speaking to me of the Judge—one who knew him well as a lawyer and as a man : " His true greatness was his character ; " and he was right. That was solid granite. It stood for a half a century before the public, simple, grand, invulnerable. It was a felt power in the jury box, in public assemblies, in the church, in the street, in social and domestic life. It put on no airs, was heralded by no trumpet. It stood before the world a human fact, accepted and trusted of all men. His opinions were sometimes minority opinions, but he was always majority. The man was never defeated, for no voting force could overthrow his moral supremacy.

In the year 1838, Mr. Skinner was appointed, by his early friend, Governor Marcy, to the office of Judge of the Eighth Circuit, who, at that time, had equity jurisdiction as Vice-Chancellor. There was an universal desire on the part of the Bar of the district that he would accept the position, but he declined it. President Pierce appointed him United States District Attorney for the Northern District of New York, which he also declined.

In 1846, he was appointed Judge of the County Court of Wyoming by the Governor, under the new Constitution, an office which he held a few months until the election. He was one of the first victims of the elective judiciary system. He continued the practice of his profession·until about 1860, when he removed to Buffalo.

The political side of the life of Judge Skinner is not without interest. The address of Mr. Fillmore, from which I have quoted, shows how highly he was valued as a legislator. He was elected to the New York Assembly for the sessions of 1827, 1828 and 1829. This was his last position in an elective office of a political character. The question is naturally asked, why he, with his gift of popular eloquence, and his adaptation to legislative and executive trusts, remained in private life through almost half a century of stormy controversy and struggle over constitutional, social and domestic questions, some of which were settled at last before the highest, the grandest tribunal ever invoked to vindicate the rights of man or the honor of nations. Did he retire voluntarily, a dreamy philosopher, or a morbid cynic, with no spirit for the fray, and with no tastes or ambition for statesmanship? On the contrary, he took a deep interest in all the politics of his time. He entertained most positive opinions upon all national questions, maintained them in all national canvasses, and was not without ambition. Indeed, I think that while he realized how much he had won by his constancy to his profession, he had a somewhat regretful feeling that, while in his prime, and when politics were specially attractive to men of his character and ability, he had no broad public career. It was not the *eclat* which may follow such a career, which he valued at its worth, no more, that attracted him, but the opportunity of public service. That opportunity he valued, and while no man with so much deserving and capability could be more unassuming, he had not been without an honorable ambition to impress his thought and character upon the law and policy of the country. If this be a weakness, it is the weakness of most able men at some period of their lives, who live in the stimulating atmosphere of democratic institutions. Why, then, was not this ambition gratified?

During the period of Mr. Skinner's service in the Legislature, a new element appeared in Western New York politics, a sort of Nile inundation, breaking up and sweeping away all old political organizations. I refer to Anti-Masonry. It took the form of a political party, and from the start was at the white heat of popular passion. The tide kept rapidly rising, and floated out on the sea of popular favor all the successful men of that generation in the career of politics in Western New York. To be an Anti-Mason was to be in the realm of possibilities for any position within the gift of the local constituency. To be of the opposition was to be whelmed under a flood of majorities which made hopeless, almost down to the present day, all its political aspirations through popular election.

It is not surprising that a party which came out as a whirlwind should aspire even to national ascendancy. But as it was local in its origin, and was the child of outraged feeling, rather than of a political idea, it shared the fate of every political organization in this country which is not based upon party traditions, or does not involve a national policy. It lasted long enough, in localities, to place several men in public relations who continued to occupy and honor them, long after the organization had been absorbed in the national opposition to the Democratic party.

It is a noticeable fact, both in the history of England and this country, that every attempt to found a new and permanent political party upon a sentiment, or upon a question of morals or of religion, has failed. There have been temporary departures from traditional organizations upon some new question, as in the case of the repeal of the corn laws in England, but with the attainment of the end, the new combination has dissolved and sought afresh its old associations.

In the United States, a country of few traditions, and no aristocratic institutions, and where so many constitutional questions have been settled by the courts, or by war, the law of the future development of parties does not appear on the surface. The democratic tendency of the age is so strong, that a reactionary party powerful enough to contest with the dominant idea for supremacy, seems a long way off. The time is not favorable for purely personal parties, and the country is too full of talent and aspirations, to have public interest monopolized by one or two men, as in the times of Jackson and Clay. I suspect that that law of party development will be found to exist here, in a large degree, as it long has existed in England, in the inheritable character of political associations, and upon the principle of systematic opposition. I should certainly regard a strong proof of the sound political condition of the country, the fact that opposition to any existing administration rested, in the main, upon the principle of such systematic opposition, so perpetuating a party, vigilant, ever ready to take advantage of the mistakes of its rival, and ever eager to supplant it and abide the same test of hostile scrutiny. But to return from this episode into which I have been led.

Mr. Skinner, as we shall see hereafter, was an intense conservative. His father was a Mason, and that fact powerfully influenced him. He could not be floated off on any impulsive tide, and he would not hold an organization responsible for a crime, atrocious as it was, of a few individual members. He united with the opposition to the Anti-Masonic party, and when the Anti-Masonic was merged in the Whig party, his attitude remained unchanged in the Democratic organization. The result was that the standard 3,000 majority in "Old Genesee," Anti-Masonic and Whig for forty years, was as Ossa on Pelion, and both on Atlas, over the hopes and candidacy of every man of the minority for political promotion.

Mr. Skinner was often the candidate of his party for high honors, but the contest was always a forlorn hope; and he led it with characteristic courage and devotion.

Mr. Skinner constitutionally was a conservative. This temperament, which led him to sympathize little with revolutionary movements in Church or State, gave the tone to all his public action. To stand in the ancient ways, to adhere to old compacts, to maintain the ancient reverences, and to heave the lead every inch of the way before venturing on an unknown deep, was the law of his nature. During all the revolutionary movement in his own Church, in 1837, and on all the exciting questions which occupied the public thought during the quarter of a century previous to the war, he was a conservative every day and every minute of that long controversy. And, when that is said, we have simply stated that his action was in obedience to that centripetal principle which is an element as essential for the safety of the Church and the State,

as it is for the harmony of the planetary system. I suppose
it is vain to expect that the radical element, without which
there would be little social progress, and stagnation would be
the reigning law, will ever be at one with its balancing conservative force, or that either will ever recognize the other but
as a foe. Both are right in themselves, both are wrong in
their estimate of each other. Each obeys the law of its nature divinely implanted, and between the two society finds
the middle path of safety.

While Judge Skinner was of this type of character, his
conservatism was rational and practical. He always ac-
quiesced in the final result of the controversy of opinions,
and was among the earliest to seek to adjust institutions to
the new idea. I have referred to the revolutionary movement in the Presbyterian Church in 1837, one of the results of
that "irrepressible conflict" between the spirit of the past
and the spirit of the present, of which our restless century
has been so fruitful. He was a Presbyterian of the old
school. He could be nothing else during the controversy.
But when time and events indicated that the largest good
would result from the reunion of the two bodies, he was of
the foremost in preparing the way for it, and no voice in the
ecclesiastical assemblies was more positive than his in urging
that consummation. I well remember his enthusiasm over the
reunion after his return from the General Assembly, when the
final action was taken. He told me the story with deep emotion. He dramatized before my mind the scene in the Assembly, its glowing oratory, its rapture and enthusiasm, its spirit
of Christian sacrifice and devotion. The occasion was to him
a Mount of Vision from which he saw the future conquests over
sin and evil, through the united power of the Church he loved.
While there was great firmness, there was no pride of opinion
in his nature. What might have appeared obstinacy to those
who did not know him well, was but the force of conviction.

I was desirous of embodying in this paper a sketch of Mr. Skinner's social and private life as it unfolded and was revealed to friendship during his residence in Wyoming. The Reverend J. E. Nassau, of Warsaw, long his intimate friend, has kindly furnished me his recollections in the following letter:

Hon. James O. Putnam:

Dear Sir,--In contributing a few recollections to your historical sketch of the late Hon. John B. Skinner, I have no need to linger upon his standing as a lawyer at the Bar, or say how highly his professional skill as an advocate was prized and sought after. This service others will render.

In Wyoming county, where he resided until his removal to Buffalo, his name and influence were prominent, his abilities cheerfully recognized, and his reputation stainless. He was as useful as he was capable, for his influence, which was great and widespread, was judiciously and happily directed. He was thoroughly identified with the civil, religious and educational interests of this thriving section of Western New York.

He was long an active officer in the Presbyterian Church of Wyoming, and often sat as ruling elder in Presbytery, Synod and General Assembly, serving in responsible positions and on important committees in church, courts and literary institutions; and for twenty years, until he left the county, he was the efficient President of the Wyoming County Bible Society. In all these and similar relations, his time, counsels, gifts and advocacy were constantly sought and freely given. The services of none were more useful or acceptable. An earnest friend of temperance and African colonization, he did much by example and generous effort to advance these and kindred causes of benevolence.

He was a man of decided convictions and settled judgments, sure to be a leading spirit, a positive factor, in whatever associations he held a place. Everybody that knew him at all, knew where Judge Skinner stood on great questions of the hour. And yet, though his views were well matured and firmly adhered to, and he far from vacillating, he was courteous in their expression. In his religious beliefs and preferences, a decided Presbyterian, he had a large heart and exhibited an eminently catholic spirit.

He was not only a man of ability and culture, but a Christian gentleman in all his impulses, speech and bearing towards others. He delighted to exercise hospitality, and have his friends gather around him. Associates were not kept at arm's length, but were admitted to his generous confidence. He possessed traits of character, qualities of mind and heart, and cultivated attainments that greatly endeared him to friends and acquaintances. Approachable, easy of access, he was capable of greatly attaching others to himself. And how heartily he cherished the friendships with which God had enriched him, well all we remember. His social intimacies were very pleasant, and embraced all ages and various classes. He was a man for others to lean on—true, sympathetic and strong. He drew others to him by his unaffected cordiality, earnest sympathies and affable manners. As to his domestic life and relations, I need hardly say that they were singularly attractive. He knew what the joys, sympathies and refinements of a Christian home were ; and to swell the fund of domestic happiness brought his own affluent contributions of piety, culture, fidelity and love.

He was a person of the finest sensibilities, that manifested themselves continually in his domestic, Christian, and professional life and intercourse. I have often see him profoundly affected and moved even to tears in religious meetings and public addresses, and even in common conversation upon topics that greatly interested him. And nothing took deeper hold of his emotion than the grand elemental truths of the Bible, the permanent interests of the Church, the sorrows and joys of friends, or the vital issues of the country.

He was a good, guileless man, whose works follow him—a man of pure motives, thoroughly conscientious and honest in all his dealings, of blameless exemplary life, a pattern of integrity.

His name will long be held in honor, and his memory warmly cherished in this and adjacent counties, where his presence was ever welcome, and where so large a part of his active life was passed, and his influence was so beneficent.

Very truly yours,   J. E. NASSAU.

WARSAW, N. Y., February 12, 1873.

Mr. Nassau has spoken of the broadness of Mr. Skinner's religious nature. It was one of the most beautiful of his characteristics. Devoted as he was to the faith and interests of his own branch of the Church, he was without sectarian narrowness, and wherever he found the act and spirit of divine worship, he gave it his Christian sympathy. As an illustration, I will relate an incident which I am sure will not be misunderstood, and I think we may profitably dwell a moment on this element of a deeply religious nature. Soon after his return from his visit abroad, in a religious meeting of a social character, he was lamenting that so few in Protestant countries were in the habit of attendance upon public worship, and contrasted the fact with what he had observed in some of the Catholic countries of Europe. He then related a scene he witnessed in a Roman Catholic Church in the Tyrol. It was the Church of St. Gilgen, which forms so pleasing a picture in Longfellow's "Hyperion." The scene was on just such a Sabbath morning as is described in that romance, "when the woods, and the clouds, and the whole village, and the very air itself seemed to pray—so silent was it everywhere." The local peasantry were all assembled in the old church, and all engaged in acts of worship and praise after the methods which many centuries have made sacred to the Tyrolese. He drew before our fancies a picture of the deep reverence and solemnity of the worshipers, and we were not left to conjecture the impression made on his own mind by this universal Sabbath religious observance. No one who listened to his words could doubt that he too was a worshiper with that humble congregation, feeling with them the common want of our humanity—rest for the soul, and communion with the Infinite Father. Their methods of worship were not his, but he looked through and beyond the externals, to the spirit they typify.

Those few words of charity and feeling, so appreciative of the greatness of the heart of God, who is not worshiped in the temple or on the mountain, but everywhere in spirit and in truth, were more eloquent words and more self-revealing, than I had ever before heard from his lips. There may be those, religious as he, who would not have been so moved, in a Roman Catholic Church, to devotional sympathy. But, surely, he is a gainer who has the wisdom that distils "the soul of goodness out of things evil," and that knows to rise from the poverty of the symbol to the wealth of the thing symbolized. Human sentiments and human sensibilities are the choral harmonies of the temple of Humanity. He who hears only discord in their commingled tones, is as one who may catch the melody of a solitary note, but has no ear for the myriad-voiced creations of Beethoven.

I have met few men in intimate relations in whom the religious element was so marked as in our friend. It seemed a part of his being. He was orthodox of the orthodox, and accepted absolutely the Evangelical type of Christianity. But his religious element, as appeared to me, upon which this superstructure of faith was builded, lay beneath all formulas, indeed all systems. He would have been religious in any age, and under any system ever formulated by devout souls. A system failing him, he would have erected the Athenian altar before which Paul stood reverently, and worshiped "the unknown God, if haply he might find him." It will be easily believed that such a nature had a ready answer to all the materialistic arguments of our time. The primal truths of religion with him, rested not upon reason, nor upon logic, nor upon any of the methods of the human understanding, but upon the instincts of the soul, its moral consciousness, and its need of God : a method of demonstration which shivers at a blow the whole fabric of materialistic negations, and is the basis on which the ultimate argument for religion must rest.

For man is "an infant crying in the night," and his hungry soul can no more find Deity by logic than the child of yester-day can by logic find the maternal fountain of its earthly life.

Wordsworth's Ode is our century's noblest interpretation of man's instinct of divinity:

> Our birth is but a sleep and a forgetting:
> The soul that rises with us, our life's Star
> Hath had elsewhere its setting
> And cometh from afar:
> Not in entire forgetfulness
> And not in utter nakedness,
> But trailing clouds of glory do we come
> From God who is our home.

Mr. Skinner was active as a reformer, ever recognizing the principle that innovation is not reform. He had no sympathy with slavery, and, as did many other good men, he at first hoped for a solution of the long unsolved American problem, in the African Colonization Society. But the time had not arrived for an historic exception to the law of the past, that social regenerations come through the shock of revolution. He was active in promoting that cause. He was an ardent friend of the temperance reform, yet never adopting extreme opinions, or favoring extreme action. While he was judge, I well remember he was a terror to violators of the license laws. There was no form of social evil that he did not oppose with the whole weight of his influence and character.

He was identified with the new State Reformatory at Warsaw. He held society responsible for its neglect of the classes who, for want of proper culture, grow up vicious, as well as neglected. He hoped little from legislation, but much from voluntary and associated action, for the elevation and reformation of the unfortunate and criminal.

When discussing the duties of society to neglected youth, he sometimes narrated an incident in his professional experience. He once volunteered to defend a lad charged with a felony clearly proved. He was born and reared amid debasing associations. Vice was his schoolmaster, his character the legitimate product of his education. He urged his acquittal upon the ground that society had failed of its duty to the accused, having never sought to raise him to a virtuous life. The defense appears sentimental, but it was successful. If the twelve did wrong as jurors, were they wholly wrong as men? This incident reveals the principle of Mr. Skinner's identification of himself rather with measures of reform of criminal youth, than with those which seek the repression of crime by vigorous punishment. Was he not right? Can there be any doubt that the Children's Aid Society of New York, which annually transfers thousands of youths, maturing in the gutters and hells of that city, for lives of crime, to homes of industry and virtue in the West, has been worth to society, as an educator, more than a thousand prisons?

When we remember the barbarism of the criminal code of fifty years ago, and the inhumanity of public sentiment in relation to poor and neglected children, let us not doubt the progress of the spirit of Christianity. "Neither do I condemn thee, go and sin no more," is the ideal of that enthusiasm of humanity which seeks the repression of youthful crime through moral instrumentalities, rather than by the pillory, the whipping post, and the chain gang. It would not abolish the criminal code, but it would humanize it, and render less necessary its execution.

Mr. Skinner was as widely identified with educational interests as any man in Western New York. He was for many years a Trustee of the Geneseo Academy, and during nearly his entire residence in Wyoming a Trustee of Middlebury Academy. He was also a Trustee of the Ingham Institute at Le Roy.

It may be a surprise to some to learn that Mr. Skinner, many years before his residence in Buffalo, actively interested himself in the enterprise to establish here a university of high rank. He made repeated journeys for consultation on the subject, and was much disappointed when Rochester took the lead of us, and founded its now flourishing college. He never abandoned his idea. Among the last conversations I had with him, he spoke of our State Normal School as the nucleus of a future university. When I called his attention to the fact that commercial towns had not generally proved favorable to the growth of universities, he abated nothing from his confidence, but found, as he thought, in the reciprocal influence of commerce and learning, an argument for so associating them.

This enumeration of his official relations will realize to us that his activity here, in connection with public institutions, was no new-born zeal, but the habit and principle of the most active part of his career.

In 1860, Mr. Skinner removed from Wyoming to Buffalo. We can hardly realize what a struggle this break up of old associations cost him. The quiet and repose of his beautiful country home and its surroundings, identified with his tastes and affections as they were, had become a part of his being. His local attachments were very strong. The very trees he planted grew up as friends to him. It was several years after he purchased his Buffalo property, before he could bring himself to the point of changing his residence. Once he sold his Wyoming home preparatory to the removal, but he was so unhappy at seeing it pass to other hands, that he repurchased it, and deferred for a considerable period his final coming to Buffalo. But after his retirement from the active duties of his profession, he made our city his residence.

What he was among us, from that time to his death, is a part of the history of our charitable, religious and educational institutions. He united himself with the Calvary Church, of which he was a ruling officer. At the time of his death he was President of the Buffalo General Hospital, a member of the Board of Education of the Presbyterian Church,

President of the New York State Asylum for the Blind
at Batavia, President of the Buffalo State Normal School,
Vice-President of the Reformatory in Warsaw, President of
the Erie County Bible Society, a Trustee of the Buffalo
Female Academy, and a Trustee of the Buffalo City Savings Bank.

His was not an idle old age. His life and talents he held
to be sacred trusts, and for the ten years of his Buffalo
residence, except an interlude of eighteen months abroad, he
devoted his leisure to the duties of a useful citizenship.

It is fresh to our recollection that he occupied himself for
weeks, not very long before his decease, in endeavoring to
persuade us to do ourselves good by providing for the payment of a paltry debt of a few thousand dollars—a dead
weight on the neck of our hospital. His success, though not
complete, was as near to completeness as any charity enterprise can be with us, which is not under the auspices of woman.
She alone can work financial miracles for charity, and in her
hopeful vocabulary there is no such word as fail. Happily
the hospital is now her ward.

In 1867 he made a visit to Europe with his family. I doubt
if it ever falls to the lot of an American traveler abroad to
enjoy more than he did. Europe with its art, its culture, its
incarnation of that past with which America, so fresh, so self-
asserting, so purely the creation of the hopeful, restless,
revolutionary present, has so little sympathy, kept all his
enthusiasm in constant glow. Almost every day was to him
as a new creation bringing with it the gladness of a fresh
inspiration.

It was while abroad that a great sorrow cast its shadow
over the heart and home of our friend. His only daughter
and child, and only grand-child, died while the family were in
Switzerland. It is not for us to lift the veil of that sorrow,
and I leave its heavy folds untouched.

He returned with the other members of his family in December, 1868, to resume his labors in the many spheres of beneficent action to which the public had called him, labors never suspended except by his last sickness and death.

Of the personal characteristics of Mr. Skinner, one of the most marked was his habit of incarnating, so to speak, in himself every interest that commanded his sympathy. Whatever represented his opinions was invested with an almost sacred character. This was true of his Church, ever an object of interest and affection. It was true of his party, which to him became personified in its leaders who had his confidence. To attack it was to attack them and to challenge their wisdom, their integrity, or their patriotism. Their honor he made his own. He was an enthusiast. A speech that much interested him was always "eloquent." A sermon, which on a different temperament would make little impression, often profoundly impressed him. Sympathy was the touchstone that transmuted everything into gold. This temperament gave a warm coloring to many a sky which had been leaden to other natures. I speak of his later years, for during his middle life he was a great sufferer from nervous depression, but this had all passed away before he came among us, and we were accustomed to look at his face as the sign of cheer and hope, so beaming was it with kindliness and joy.

Great simplicity and dignity of character were combined in him. He was proud in the sense in which honor and conscious integrity have a right to be proud, but his was a latent pride, a covert fortress for the defence of character and self-respect. There was something of the old chivalry in his nature. He paid reverence where it was due. There was ever in his bearing that courtesy and regard for the sensibility of others which constitute the highest charm of social manners. His ordinary method of speech was subdued and gentle. Baseness would rouse him from his usual calm, and then it was made to feel the force of his indignation. He was faithful to the obligations of friendship, and to old friends he clung with romantic attachment.

He was twice married. In 1830, to Catharine, only daughter of Mr. Richard M. Stoddard, of Le Roy. She died in 1832, leaving no children. He was again married in 1837 to Sarah A., daughter of Mr. Henry G. Walker, of Wyoming. Their only child was the late Mrs. Josiah Letchworth. He died June 6, 1871, after a few weeks illness.

His last years, with the exception of the single sorrow to which I have alluded, were serene and happy. He had won all which professional eminence and purity of character could secure to him—reputation, ample fortune, private esteem, and public respect. His life had been widely useful, his example pure.

Death found him amid the sweets of friendship and the ministrations of love, his pathway to eternity luminous with the light of religion.

APPENDIX.

The great importance Judge Skinner attached to Bible distribution, and the interest he felt in it, may be seen in the following extracts from an address made by him at an Anniversary Meeting of the American Bible Society, held at the Bible House in New York :

(From published Reports of the American Bible Society.)

On motion of Hon. John B. Skinner, of Wyoming County, N. Y.,

Resolved,—That our free institutions, and those moral enterprises designed to improve the condition of the race, sprang from the Bible, and without its influence they cannot be sustained.

The influence of the Bible, observed Judge S., upon the destiny of man as a social being—the tendency of its teachings to develop a knowledge of his rights and duties, and to prepare him to understand and to sustain the responsibilities of a citizen in the government of the people is a topic not unworthy of consideration upon an occasion like this.

In this view it may not be uninteresting or unprofitable to trace the history of our free institutions, and to examine the causes which have produced and thus far sustained them. I refer not now to that noble vindication of the rights of man, to which our fathers pledged their lives, their fortunes, and their sacred honor; nor to that revolutionary struggle which gave us a name as one of the nations of the earth : for these, and the blood and treasure which they cost, would have been as unavailing as other more recent struggles for liberty, but for that regard for the Bible and its sanctions which characterized these movements. The deep convictions, the uncompromising principles, which had induced the Puritans, more than a century and a half before, to encounter persecution and banishment, and every peril, for the rights of conscience and the freedom of religious opinion, had produced a spirit of inquiry into the nature of civil government and the principles of popular liberty, which prepared them to comprehend and to assert the new and startling truth --that the will of the people is the only just foundation of civil government.

The early settlers of this country, who had fled from religious despotism, had been thorough students of the Bible, and were deeply imbued with the doctrines of the Gospel. Before the settlement at Jamestown or at Plymouth our present translation had been finished and was generally circulated, and all its teachings were familiar to those Puritans who would admit no authority but the Bible, and allow no priest, nor parliament, nor king, nor hierarchy to interpret it.

The venerable Robinson, in his parting words to the embarking Pilgrims, as if animated with a prophetic view of the future destiny of his flock, with the deep earnestness and emotion of a spiritual father, pronounced the solemn and authoritative injunction, so well remembered: " I charge you, before God and his blessed angels, . . . that you be ready to receive whatever of truth shall be made known to you from the written word of God."

It was in the cabin of the Mayflower, on the desolate coast of New England, and before a foot-print had been made upon the shore, that the memorable instrument of government was signed by every adult male person, which event a distinguished historian has pronounced " the birth of popular constitutional liberty, where humanity recovered its rights and instituted government on the basis of equal laws for the general good."

The mass of mankind knew no liberties except such as were wrung from the grasp of hereditary power; they looked to royal charters for the measure of their rights and the rule of their duty; but these Puritans, nurtured in the sentiments of Luther and Calvin, and in the school of intolerance, had searched the oracles of God as the only admitted standard of authority, the only acknowledged arbiter of their rights.

We must look back to the commencement of the Christian era—

to the doctrines which the Son of God proclaimed on the plains of Palestine—for the first dawn of light upon the rights of man. "The blind see, the lame walk, the deaf hear, and to the poor the Gospel is preached," were the evidences which He put forth of His mission, and of His divinity. Philosophers and sages have studied, and labored and taught, but all their theories had respect to the priviledged, the high-born, and the prosperous. It was Jesus of Nazareth who first put forth the claims of a common brotherhood, and enforced the duties of a common humanity. Disregarding the artificial distinctions which the world reverenced, He lifted up the poor, the neglected and the friendless, and laid the foundation of those principles of reciprocal justice and popular liberty so distinctly visible in the democracy of the Pilgrims, and the Declaration of Independence adopted by the Revolutionary fathers.

Regard for the Bible, and reverence for its precepts, have marked every period of our early history. It was in the darkest hour of our Revolution, amidst the cares and the anxieties and the dangers of the fearful conflict, and a few days before Congress were driven from Philadelphia, that a proposition was considered to supply the country with Bibles, and a resolution passed to import twenty thousand copies at the public expense.

Thus, while the French Revolution rejected the Bible and its Author, abolished the Sabbath, and wrote over the gateway to the grave, "Death is an eternal sleep;" our fathers raised this Book above every other standard, and inscribed upon it those words which the Christian emperor is said to have seen written upon the cross hung out from the skies, "In hoc vince."

At a later period, after the struggle was over and peace was restored, when the Convention assembled to form a Constitution, to secure the fruits of that contest to us and those who should come after us, such was the diversity of interest and conflict of opinion, so numerous were the theories advanced, that the momentous objects of the meeting hung in doubt and uncertainty, when the venerable Franklin a name not associated with the strictest Puritans, representing a constituency far removed from the rock on which they landed, and the spot consecrated by their toil and sufferings, arose and addressed that body in a speech which has been preserved, and which I beg leave to read as a happy illustration of the sentiment of this resolution.

"*Sir:* In the beginning of the contest with Britain, when we were sensible of danger, we had daily prayers in this room for the Divine protection. Our prayers, sir, were heard and they were graciously answered. All of us who were engaged in the struggle must have observed frequent instances of a superintending Providence in our favor. To that kind Providence we owe this happy opportunity of consulting in peace on the means of establishing our future national felicity : and have we now forgotten that powerful Friend? or do we imagine that we no longer need His assistance? I have lived, sir, a long time. and the longer I live, the more convincing proofs I see of this truth —that God governs the affairs of men ; and if a sparrow cannot fall without His notice, is it probable that an empire can rise without His aid? We have been assured, sir, in the Sacred Writings that ' Except the Lord build the house, they labor in vain that build it :' and I firmly believe this, and I also believe, that without His concurring aid we shall succeed no better than the builders of the tower of Babel. We shall be divided by our little partial, local interests ; our projects will be confounded, and we ourselves shall become a reproach and a by-word down to future ages ; and what is worse, mankind may hereafter, from this unfortunate instance, despair of establishing governments by human wisdom, and leave it to chance, war and conquest. I therefore beg leave to move that henceforth prayers, imploring the assistance of heaven and its blessings upon our deliberations, be held in this assembly every morning, before we proceed to business."

These were the sentiments of the founders of our republic ; upon this rock was our fabric erected ; and if we are true to the faith they have delivered to us, and follow in the paths they have marked, our liberties are safe.

If our civil liberties can thus be traced to the teachings of the Gospel, as illustrated and exemplified in the character and policy of our Puritan fathers,—if we must look to their principles for the germ of our civil privileges and the elements of our greatness,—who can estimate the value of the Bible, and the importance of the work in which we are engaged, as a means of perpetuating these blessings ?

Let this volume be circulated—let it be carried to every house—let its truths and precepts find place in the hearts of our wide-spread population— every patriotic sentiment will be awakened, every noble aspiration strengthened, and every social virtue cherished ; it will disarm prejudice, dispel superstition, subdue the passions and link together a mighty people from every nation, and kindred and tongue, in the bonds of peace, in the love of man and in the fear of God.

But I have touched only a single point—such a view of this subject would be like that relief which should take the helpless, drowning man from the fatal wreck, and carry him within view of the cheering light, and within sound of the glad voices of sympathy and kindred, and leave him there to die unblest. I have not referred to the power of the Gospel to break the fetters in which pride, and avarice and selfishness have bound up the charities of the soul ; nor to those fountains of benevolence which this week commemorates, and which, springing from this source, have sent forth their gushing waters over the dry earth, producing moral beauty and verdure and loveliness. I have not alluded to that noble institution in the father-land, whose jubilee has just been celebrated, and which has shed its radiance over every clime, and whose light, mingling with ours, beams from those bright spots indicated on your missionary map, which a kindred institution has rescued from the desert. I have not spoken of that boon of sympathy and brotherhood which has reclaimed the drunkard, and sought out the abandoned, and carried the hopes of life to the lost. These are fruits of that Tree of Life whose leaves are for the healing of the nations.

Nay, this influence is the voice of the Son of God in the sepulchre of Lazarus. It penetrates the grave, and rescues its tenants from corruption and the worm ; it clothes them with a robe of spotless righteousness : it furnishes them with a passport to that city which hath foundation, to those joys which "eye hath not seen, nor ear heard, nor hath entered into the heart of man to conceive."

www.ingramcontent.com/pod-product-compliance
Lightning Source LLC
Chambersburg PA
CBHW030008030726
47499CB00008B/2956